More Praise for PALO ALTO

"The stories are raw and funny-sad, and they capture with perfect pitch the impossible exhilaration, the inevitable downbeat-ness, and the pure confusion of being an adolescent. . . . Franco has a flair for creating these stopped moments that lift a story from its specific setting into a universal place, so that particular meanings resonate out from themselves and redouble their effect."

—*Elle*

"Delightfully coarse, riffing dialogue that hones in on subjects like race and sex, love and violence . . . Compelling and gutsy."

—*Vogue*

"Franco writes with such deep empathy and affinity that one has to wonder if he lived this life."

—*USA Today*

"You'll be able to pick out Franco's influences: Raymond Carver's tight-lipped stoicism; the sun-streaked disaffection of *Less Than Zero* . . . Hubert Selby Jr.'s *Last Exit to Brooklyn*. . . . He excels at dialogue."

—Salon.com

"In 'I Could Kill Someone' especially, about a high schooler's deliberations over murdering a bully, there is an element of sympathy for the tormented narrator that makes his thought process real and frightening. . . . Franco is a serious writer."

—*The Wall Street Journal*

"[Franco's] economic construction seems so simple through-out, but the stories end up approaching profundity. These stories were not published because James Franco is a movie star but because they are good. He makes the difficult appear simple, which only a good writer can do."

—*Booklist*

"The collection exhibits a . . . clear sense of purpose. . . . It is, in short, literature."

—*New York Journal of Books*

"It's the harsh humor that surprises in these stories—that and the observations that show James Franco to be an original and simpatico voice finely tuned to the territory. These quotable, unsettling stories stay with you; they seem to change the ions in a room."

—Amy Hempel

"James Franco's stories are raw, unsettling, and delectable. Each articulates a very American yearning within a dystopic suburban landscape of shifting sexuality, class, and race. They are both really scary and fun to read."

—Darcey Steinke, author of *Easter Everywhere*

"Franco's talent is unmistakable, his ambition profound. He has taken the twin subjects of suburban Palo Alto and American adolescence and made them as scary and true as they must be. This is a book to be inhaled more than once, with delight and admiration, with unease and pure enjoyment. As a writer, he's here to stay."

—Gary Shteyngart, author of *Super Sad True Love Story*

"James Franco's chilling stories seem too true for comfort. The characters in *Palo Alto* navigate off a moral compass so smashed, they bruise everything they touch. Franco's intense artistry swarms all over this gripping book. Think Bret Easton Ellis, Dennis Cooper, Kathy Acker. Or better yet, just think James Franco."

—Ben Marcus, author of *Notable American Women*

"These rough messages torn from the notebook of angry youth just make us want to ask James Franco to say it ain't so. These angular stories read like dispatches from the edge of civilization: all the young people hurting and denying it, denying connection, denying their hope for anything but tonight, the next thing. James Franco does not blink as he offers us these stories—and it is hard for us to look away."

—Ron Carlson, author of *The Signal*

"James Franco is a writer of skill and sensitivity whose depiction of cruelty and neglect, of amusement and loneliness, of longing and being lost—of the pains and chaos of adolescence—is original and impressive. He manages to depict the numbingly stupid and dangerous behavior of teenagers and make it amazingly amusing then suddenly deeply sad."

—Susan Minot, author of *Rapture*

PALO ALTO

stories

James Franco

Scribner

New York   London   Toronto   Sydney   New Delhi

SCRIBNER

A Division of Simon & Schuster, Inc.
1230 Avenue of the Americas
New York, NY 10020

First Scribner trade paperback media tie-in edition May 2014

SCRIBNER and design are registered trademarks of The Gale Group, Inc., used under license by Simon & Schuster, Inc., the publisher of this work.

For information about special discounts for bulk purchases, please contact Simon & Schuster Special Sales at 1-866-506-1949 or business@simonandschuster.com.

The Simon & Schuster Speakers Bureau can bring authors to your live event. For more information or to book an event contact the Simon & Schuster Speakers Bureau at 1-866-248-3049 or visit our website at www.simonspeakers.com.

Designed by Carla Jayne Jones
Cover art by P+A

Manufactured in the United States of America

10   9   8   7   6   5   4   3   2   1

Library of Congress Control Number: 2010032932

ISBN 978-1-4391-6314-6
ISBN 978-1-4767-7838-9 (pbk)
ISBN 978-1-4391-7572-9 (ebook)

The story "Jack-O'" first appeared in *Esquire* magazine in a slightly altered form.

Photographs on pp. 226–30 appear courtesy of Sammy Bandini Films, LLC. All rights reserved. Photographs on 226 and 230 by David James Swanson; 229 (bottom) by Sebastian Pardo; 227 (bottom) and 228 (bottom) by Keegan Allen; 227 (top) and 228 (top) by Grear Patterson; 227 (middle) and 229 (top) by Gia Coppola.

To the teachers
Ian R. Wilson
Mona Simpson
Amy Hempel
Michael Cunningham
Jenny Offill

There is hardly a single action that we perform in that phase which we would not give anything, in later life, to be able to annul. Whereas what we ought to regret is that we no longer possess the spontaneity which made us perform them. In later life we look at things in a more practical way, in full conformity with the rest of society, but adolescence is the only period in which we learn anything.

—*Within a Budding Grove,*
Remembrance of Things Past

Contents

Contents

PALO ALTO I

Halloween

Ten years ago, my sophomore year in high school, I killed a woman on Halloween.

I had been drinking at Ed Sales's house all afternoon, which I wasn't supposed to be doing because I was on probation. The probation rules said I was only allowed to drive to school and then right back home after school was out. But it was six months since I'd been arrested for being a minor under the influence, and my parents had become lax about the driving rules. On that Halloween Tuesday, instead of going home, I took some friends over to Ed's and we all got drunk.

His father was a mathematics professor at Stanford and his mother was a nurse, and neither of them came home until at least six but usually seven. His professor father had a great liquor cabinet. I had my first drink there when I was thirteen, and in the three years since then we had been taking from his cupboard and putting water back into the bottles. We could never get much from any one bottle because it would be too obvious; so we would take a little from all the bottles and mix everything into a punch like the bums did in *Cannery Row*. I like that we did that, I liked thinking that we were like Mack and the boys, even though the punch tasted horrible. We'd usually mix it with grape juice, but it wouldn't help much.

We were all sitting in the backyard on a little picnic table that you might find at a park. His dad probably took it from the dump. He was always doing weird stuff like that to save money. Ed did it too, like scraping the mold off old bread and then eating it. His dad was a mathematics professor who smoked a pipe, every night. His teeth were yellow and crooked and horrible. Ed had a little pipe and he smoked tobacco with his dad at night. Ed was half Korean and half white because his mother was Korean and his dad was white from Gary, Indiana.

Outside, we were smoking weed in Ed's little tobacco pipe. We were all planning on going to Alice Wolfe's house later for the Halloween party, and we were getting ourselves revved up. I picked a fight with Nick Dobbs. I had seen him hanging around my girlfriend, Susan, and I didn't like it. I spotted them a couple times laughing in the corner of the library at school. I probably wouldn't have cared if he had been just one of those theater dorks that she was always planning events with, but he wasn't. He was a handsome skateboarder, and I had enough of the alcohol punch in me to start something.

"I heard you and Susan did acid. Why did you give my girlfriend acid?"

"She wanted it."

His eyes actually looked worried. It was not the reaction I was expecting. I suddenly felt powerful and a little bad for him at the same time. I probably couldn't have asked for a better reaction because I really wasn't a fighter, and this way, because he looked scared, I had beat him without having to fight him. I didn't like to see people intimidated, but this guilt made me turn meaner because I told him to apologize, and when he did, I demanded that he say it louder so that everyone could hear. I was pushing it a little and I could see him consider just taking a swing at me, but he apologized again slightly louder. Jack spoke up.

"What the fuck do you care, Ryan? She does acid and other drugs all the time, with all of us."

Well, I didn't like that. Funny how new facts pop up and make you doubt that there's any goodness in life. Everyone pretends to be normal and be your friend, but underneath, everyone is living some other life you don't know about, and if only we had a camera on us at all times, we could go and watch each other's tapes and find out what each of us was really like. But then you'd have to watch girls go poo and boys trying to go down on themselves.

Then Ed's Korean mom came home. She was only about four foot ten, but we all got scared anyway. We heard the front door close inside the house, and Ed said, "My mom's home!" And we grabbed most of the cups and someone grabbed the punch and Ed grabbed his pipe and we all scrambled over the fence and jumped into my car. It was a Honda Accord I'd inherited from my father when things were better between us, and it was pretty small for eight people. There were two others in the front besides me and five in the back. Jack's elbow was in my face, and when I looked in the rearview, the backseat was a jumble of arms and torsos and heads up against the ceiling. Nick wasn't in the car. He ran off somewhere to go and cry, I guess.

I raced out of there. It wasn't time for Alice's party so we had to find a place to go. The sun was going down, and there were already trick-or-treaters out with their parents. Everyone started getting rambunctious. It made it hard to drive with all the yelling and Jack's elbow in my face.

"Get that thing out of my face!"

Jack just laughed because there wasn't much he could do with his elbow. Everyone was talking very loudly, and the people that had saved their cups were trying to drink their punch and were spilling it all over the car. Then for some reason everyone started chanting, "Fuck Alice Wolfe, fuck Alice Wolfe, fuck the Wolfe!" We didn't know why we were saying it, at least I didn't, but it was really funny, and some of the guys were howling and everyone was feeling good from the drinks and about the escape and about the night ahead.

For some reason I was still driving fast. As if we were racing somewhere. I guess I just wanted to get this octopus of bodies out of the car as soon as possible, but it was also more fun to drive faster, as if we were really having a crazy adventure. I used to think of these escapades around the neighborhood as good life experience.

We decided to go to Eleanor Park to lie low before the party. There was a little community garden in the back of the park where people could grow their own vegetables, and there were some picnic tables there just like the one in Ed's backyard. We all sat down and continued what we had been doing at Ed's house. Ed went over and started picking baby tomatoes and carrots from the garden. They were small but tasted really good, and the carrots were soft and buttery tasting. Ivan went over and started kicking a trellis down, and everyone laughed because his foot went through it.

It was a simple existence, when I look back on it now. I have friends who grew up in New York City, and the stories they have from their childhoods are amazing. Full of color and culture and danger. I envy them.

At about eight we went to Alice Wolfe's party. We had finished the punch in the park, and everyone was feeling even happier. The Wolfe chant started up again, but this time it was slurred. Now that we were close to the house, the chant began to take on meaning for me. It meant that we had little respect for Alice Wolfe and her friends. Yes, they were the prettiest, most popular girls in our class, but they weren't that pretty. And our chant meant that we were going to dominate them. We were going to go over there and do our best to get them alone and fuck them.

We had decided to go as monkeys. We had identical monkey masks that we'd stashed in the trunk. All eight of us wore one so no one could tell us apart. At Alice's it worked out great. It broke the ice because we could act as stupidly as we liked, and we ended up making the girls laugh a lot more than

7

they usually did. I had a few more beers, and then I found myself talking on the back porch with Sandy Cooper.

"I know it's you, Ryan."

"Nooooo it's naaaaht." I was using a deep, doofusy kind of voice like Baloo from the *Jungle Book* movie.

"I'll pretend it's not you so if I get caught I won't get beat up by Susan."

"Whoooooo's Suuusaaan?"

"Shut up, Ryan."

I took the monkey mask off, and we made out for a bit in the backyard. Then I figured that I had better call Susan because I said I was going to. She was going to a different, less cool party with her girlfriends because they weren't invited to Alice's. I needed to come up with an excuse not to meet her. I told Sandy to wait, and I went inside to use the phone.

I called Susan at her house.

"Took you long enough," she said.

"What?"

"You were supposed to call me two hours ago."

"Sorry, we were just over at the park and there wasn't a phone around."

"Good excuse."

"It's true. So you're still at home?"

"Yeah, we're just getting our costumes on."

"Who?"

"Me and Elizabeth and Jenny and Hart and Nick."

"Nick Dobbs? What's he doing there?"

"Putting his costume on. He and Hart are going to be the guys from *A Clockwork Orange* with Terry and Pete."

"Why the fuck are you hanging out with Nick?"

"He's my friend."

"Yeah, getting real friendly in the library."

I hung up the phone. I told Jack and Ed that I was leaving, and I ran out to my car. The driveway and bushes were blurry as I ran. I got the car handle in my grip and opened the door. I got in and took off toward Susan's.

I was racing on my anger. On the righteousness of catching Nick with her. I had no clear plan for what I would do when I arrived, but I could see my fist going toward Nick's face. I had glimpses of Hart's angry face; I'd probably have to deal with him too. He was bigger than me. I'd probably have to reason with him after I kicked the shit out of Nick. I saw Susan's horrified reaction, and I felt buffeted on a hot wave of self-righteousness. The streets were fairly empty, and I accepted them as my personal roadway. My ordinary submission to traffic laws evaporated. I raced around corners without looking and shot through the phantom walls of the stoplights. The more recklessly I drove, the easier it was.

The Main Library passed on my left. I went through the red light at Embarcadero and Newell and passed Candice Brown's house on the right. Bitch, she cheated on her boyfriend too. I shot down Newell, busting through neighborhood stop signs toward Jordan Middle School. At the school I screeched through the stop sign and around the corner to the right.

There was no time to do anything about the dark figure standing in the road. The car went right at it. There was a bump and the figure disappeared underneath the car. I realized I was already pressing the brakes when the car stopped ten yards away. I put the car in Park and pressed the button for the automatic window and stuck my body out the window to look back. The figure was lying facedown on the road. There was no one else around. Just the empty school on one side of the street and on the other some sycamores in shadow. Whoever the figure was couldn't have seen what kind of car raced into her. I took the moment and drove off before she started moving.

I was driving fast again, but I obeyed the street signs now. I didn't know where to go. My rage had dissipated into a little boy's fear for his safety. I couldn't go to Susan's, and I didn't want to go home because my father would see how drunk I was; but I wanted to get the car off the street. Ed's house was close, and I drove in that direction. The flaccid monkey mask in the passenger seat looked like it was grinning. It was an object from a different time. Alice Wolfe's house and Sandy Cooper were far away. The accident had drained the life from everything that had happened earlier.

Near Ed's, I parked the car very carefully under the shadow of a large tree. I got out and forced myself to look at the front of the car. There was only a small dent on the front of the hood where the head must have hit. I didn't see any blood. I realized I was only wearing a T-shirt, and I was shivering.

I knocked on Ed's door. Inside, someone grumbled, and then, finally, there were footsteps. Ed's professor father opened the door. At first only a little, and then he saw it was me and stuck his bald lightbulb head out and smiled, showing his bad teeth.

"Why, hello, Ryan. I thought you were some late trick-or-treaters, and I was about to tell them to go screw."

"Can I come in?"

"Uhh, sure. Is everything all right?"

I was still shivering.

"Yeah, I'm just drunk and I don't want to drive right now. I don't think it would be safe."

I thought he would understand about being drunk better than my own father. My father was tired of my shit.

"Sure, come in," he said. He sat in his chair and I sat on the couch. Ed's mom wasn't there. The TV was on to the news, something about the Gulf War. Ed's dad took up his meerschaum pipe and lit it.

"Would you like to smoke? Ed usually keeps his pipe here on the bookshelf, but I don't see it. Here, I have an extra."

He picked up another old pipe and loaded it with tobacco.

"Just suck a bit while you get it started or it will go out."

I did, and inhaled sweet-tasting tobacco.

"Where's Ed?" he said.

"Oh, out with the guys, I guess."

"Chasing tail, no doubt."

This was funny because Ed wasn't the best guy with the ladies.

"Hope it works out for him," he said. "He's gone through all the tissues in the house." He laughed a high-pitched, too-big laugh. The longer I sat there, the more I calmed down. It meant no one was coming after me. My father would hardly notice the dent on the already beat-up car. I might get in a little trouble because I had kept the car and not gone home after school, but that would blow over. I would tell Susan that I got upset over Nick and went home.

After about an hour there was something on the news about the actor River Phoenix overdosing outside a club in LA. Then I decided to go.

"You sure you'll be all right?"

"Yeah, I feel okay now. Thanks, Mr. Sales."

I never told anyone about the accident. The *San Jose Mercury* ran a story about the woman the day after and so did the *Palo Alto Weekly*. She was a librarian and had been walking home from work. She lived alone.

My last couple of years of high school, I passed that corner a few times, and the little-boy terror came back. But eventually the feeling left. When I went back home from college to visit my parents, I'd drive past the corner, and it seemed like the accident only happened in a movie.

After my father died, I'd visit my mother at Christmas. One December, I passed the corner while driving my mother to the library. At first the corner didn't register. My mother was talking about the new children's book she was working on, and I was just listening to her when, halfway down the block, I remembered, "Oh yeah, that's where the accident happened."

Lockheed

Math is my dad's favorite subject. He works in Silicon Valley at IBM. He does math all day. I hate math. He makes me study with him, so I'm really good in math class, but I don't announce it because I'm a girl.

When I got to high school I didn't have friends. My best friend moved away, and I wasn't popular. I didn't go to parties. I got drunk only once, at a wedding. I puked behind a gazebo. I was with my cousin Jamie, who is gay. He goes to high school in Menlo Park, which is a five-minute drive. He is my only friend. He smokes menthol cigarettes.

After school I would go home. Me and Mom and Tim would watch *Roseanne* at the dinner table because Dad wasn't there to say no.

Then Dad would come home and we would study.

A lot of times my math tests were on Thursdays, so my dad and I would study extra long on Wednesdays, and I would miss *Beverly Hills 90210*. I never taped it.

I did so well in math class that I got this internship for the summer at Lockheed Martin. They make missiles and satellites. I was the only girl out of ten students who got selected. My dad was very excited.

He said, "Marissa, one day you and I will work together."

That summer, between my freshman and sophomore years, I worked for a Swedish guy named Jan, pronounced Yan. My job was to watch old film reels of the moon. There were hundreds. I worked in a cold, windowless basement. The reels would run from one spool to another on this old machine that looked like a tank. I was supposed to record blemishes and splices in the film. Sometimes the moon was full; sometimes it would get a little more full as I watched. Sometimes the film was scratched so badly it skipped, or it broke. I was in the basement forty hours a week. I watched so many moons.

It got so boring, I stopped looking for splices. Instead, I drew pictures on computer paper that I pulled from the recycling bin. Jan was never around, so I drew a lot. I drew rainbows, and people, and cities, and guns, and people getting shot and bleeding, and people having sex. When I got tired I just drew doodles. I tried to draw portraits of people I knew.

My family always looked ridiculous, but funny because the pictures resembled them, but not enough. Then I drew all these things from my childhood, like Hello Kitty and Rainbow Brite and My Little Pony. I drew my brother's G.I. Joes. I made the My Little Ponys kill the G.I. Joes.

I drew hundreds of pictures and they were all bad. I wasn't good at drawing. It was also a little sad to draw so much because I could see everything that was inside me. I had drawn everything I could think of. All that was inside me was a bunch of toys, and TV shows, and my family. My life was boring. I only had one kiss, and it was with my gay cousin, Jamie.

One day, Jan came down to the basement. He saw all my little drawings. He didn't say much. He picked them up and looked at them. He looked at every picture that was there. When he finished with each, he put it onto a neat pile.

He was tall and restrained, with clean, fading blond hair, combed back, with a slight wave in the front. He had a plain gold wedding band. As he looked at the pictures, I tried to imagine what he did for fun, but I couldn't. He put the last picture down on the neat stack and looked at me.

"How is Mr. Moon?" he asked. In his accent his words came out short and clean. There was a hint of warmth, but it was contained.

"I found a few scratches today," I said.

"Good," he said, and left. I didn't draw any more that day. I looked at the moon.

The next day I was back in the basement. It was almost lunchtime, and Jan came in.

"Come here," he said, and turned and walked out. I followed him down the hall and outside. We crossed the parking lot, me following him. The surface of the blacktop was melting where they had put tar to fill in the cracks. There were no trees in the parking lot and the sun was pushing hard. I followed the back of Jan's light yellow shirt and tan slacks over to his truck. It was an old, faded mustard-colored pickup that said TOYOTA in white on the back.

When I got to the truck, he was messing around with something in the stake bed. He put the back part that said TOYOTA down. On top of this, he laid out a big, black portfolio. He opened it and there were drawings inside.

"Look," he said. He stepped back, and I looked. He said, "These are mine."

They were good. They were mostly portraits. There were a bunch of portraits of a pretty woman's face, all the same woman. He was a lot better than I was.

"That's Greta, my wife," he said. "She was not my wife then, when I made them. She became my wife."

"She's very beautiful," I said. She was. Prettier than me.

"I did these when I was at school," he said. "I wanted to be artist. But it was no good. It is no good to be artist. I practiced every day, eight hours a day. Then I could draw like Michelangelo. Then what? There is already Michelangelo. I realized there was nothing more to do. In science, there is always more to learn. Always more."

I didn't look at him; I looked at his pictures. I felt very lonely. I pictured him and his wife, alone at a long table, eating some bland Swedish food, not talking. The only sounds were from the utensils hitting the plates, and the squish of their gentle chewing.

"So," he said. "You see." He reached over me and shut the portfolio to punctuate the "You see," but I didn't know what to see. Then I looked at him. He stood there and looked at me. We were so awkward.

"Okay," he said finally. "See you."

"See you," I said.

That summer, my only friend was my cousin Jamie. He was smart, and knew what he liked. He could be pretty mean behind people's backs because people were so mean to his face.

Jamie invited me to a Fourth of July party, at this Menlo girl's house, Katie Hesher. It was my first high school party. She lived on the other side of the San Francisquito Creek. It was woodsy over there. It was this big, one-story wooden house, like a fancy log cabin. We got there around nine. There were roomfuls of people. Everyone was drinking beer, mostly Keystone Light. I recognized a lot of people from my school, Paly, but I'd never seen them outside of school.

Jamie got me a beer; I opened it and held it. Jamie went off somewhere, and I sat on a couch in the living room. People came and sat on the couch, and talked, and left. I sat there for a long time. I didn't know anyone from Menlo, and I didn't know the people from my school. I sipped my beer. It was like thick, frothy urine.

I thought about Jan's Fourth of July. I imagined him going to a movie. He was with his wife, Greta. They entered the theater with their arms around each other. They were smiling.

Maybe they were going to see *Schindler's List.* They sat in the movie and ate popcorn and enjoyed it and were serious about life.

After a while, I got up and went outside. There was a mist. I walked down the long driveway, under the large syca-more trees. The noise from the party got quieter the farther I walked. At the end of the driveway, I crossed the street. On the other side was the San Francisquito Creek bed. It was very deep and steep and I could barely see the water at the bottom. It was so dark.

I still had my beer. I couldn't finish it. I took another sip, and then dumped the rest out into the dirt. The creek trickled in the black below, the bushes around me were still. I kept the can, and I walked back across the road and up the driveway. I saw a guy from my school, a water polo player named Zack Cuttle. He was standing behind one of the cars in the drive-way. I was about to say hi, but then I realized that he was prob-ably peeing. I tried to walk by discreetly. As I passed, I could see that his eyes were closed. I looked over, and I realized that he wasn't peeing; he was getting a blow job from some-one behind the car. I stood there for a second. Then I walked quickly before he saw me. I went up the stairs and back inside.

I couldn't find my cousin Jamie. I sat back on the couch, right in the middle. There were lots of people around. Every-one was talking so loudly. After a few minutes, Zack Cuttle and Stephanie Jeffs walked inside. I looked at them, and then I looked down. They went into the kitchen, where a lot of people were.

Then this guy sat next to me. Ronny Feldman. He sat right

next to me on the couch. He was a bad kid and he was hand-some. He had gone to my school but had been kicked out.

"What are you doing here?" he said.

"I came with my cousin."

"But why are you *here*?"

"I don't know," I said. He laughed. Then he grabbed my beer can and shook it a little. He laughed again because it was empty. He put it on the table.

"Here," he said, and gave me another Keystone Light. I was already feeling light-headed from the first beer.

"Thanks," I said. He was wearing a white T-shirt that was thin from being washed so many times. The neck was wasting away. His arms were thin but muscular. They had all these old scars and bruises on them. He had short, straight blond hair and a cherubic face, with a perfect nose. He was so handsome, but also like a little boy and dangerous.

I didn't know what to say, so I opened the beer and took a sip. Too big of a sip. I choked.

"Easy," he said. He patted me on the back.

He kept patting me, even after I stopped choking. I didn't stop him. He did it softly. One of his friends walked by, this black guy named Camper Williams. He had skinny arms and legs, but a fat belly. His face was like a pit bull's.

"That's fucked-up, Ronny," said Camper.

"What?" said Ronny. He stopped patting me. Camper laughed and walked away.

We sat there, and then I said, "Why did you get kicked out of school?"

"Because I broke all the windows in this asshole's car."

"Why did you do that?"

"This motherfucker, Brian Simpson, threw some eggs at me."

"Why?" I was very interested.

"Whatever. On the Sunday before, I was walking, and I saw this car drive by. Someone said something, and then I saw the car turn around . . ."

"Where?" I said.

He looked at me funnily, like who cared where it happened, and then he said, "Over on East Meadow. So they drove back and they threw eggs at me. I fucking chased them, but they were gone. I guess Brian thought I wouldn't recognize the car, but I did. So on that next Monday, I went to school at lunchtime . . ."

"You didn't go to first period?"

"No, I—no, I skipped first period." He seemed like he was laughing at me a little bit. But not in a bad way. "I just went at lunch, to fuck up his car. I smashed every window with a bat. They kicked me out for that."

"So now where do you go?"

"I went to this continuation school, Shoreline, but I got kicked out because I was the only white dude with all these black and Mexican dudes from East Palo Alto. They thought they could fuck with me, but they couldn't. They kicked me out for fighting. Now I go to this school for idiots and I'm with the *real* retards."

He was *so.* So dirty, and just moving in front of me, and cute. I was in love with him, especially because he was talking to me.

"I bet you're smart," he said. It was the best moment of my life.

Then this guy came up to him. He looked part Latino.

"What's up, little bitch?" the Latino guy said to Ronny. Ronny was calm. He looked up at the Latino guy. This guy was older.

"Fuck you," said Ronny, but softly. Then it seemed like the party got quieter.

Katie Hesher came out of the kitchen. She looked upset. She said, "Ronny, don't! Not in my parents' house."

"Come outside, little bitch," said the older guy to Ronny. The older guy looked like an ugly wolf. He had a skinny face, and pointy, uneven teeth. There were zits all over his nose. "Come outside, little Ronny," he said.

"Ronny, kick this spic's fucking ass," said someone in the crowd. Ronny stood up.

"Don't get hurt," I said. He didn't hear me. Everything was fast and scary. I sat there for a minute on the couch. Everyone else was pushing to get outside, after Ronny. I was still waiting for Ronny to finish talking. He was telling me I was smart and he was looking at me. But he was gone. It was like it hadn't happened.

I got up and squeezed onto the porch with all the people. Mist was on the front lawn. The whole party was out there. Ronny was in front of everyone. I couldn't see the Latino guy. Ronny took his shirt off. He was thin, and tough, and wiry in the mist. The guys were cheering him on. He was laughing with excitement. He had a big white smile. The other guys worked up this chant. They were saying, "Wetback attack," over and over. Ronny's older brother was there, Boris. I only knew who he was because he was a legend. He had got into more trouble than Ronny did when he was in high school. They were both Russian. I knew that. I don't know how I knew that. Boris took his shirt off too. A bunch of the guys took their shirts off. I was standing behind so many people on the porch. It started to rain a little. Their bodies were pearly in the misty rain. Their chests were flexing and their stomachs were breathing.

Then everyone was fighting. It wasn't just Ronny. All the Latino guy's friends, and Ronny's friends. There was shouting. I couldn't see Ronny; he was in the middle of everything. I saw Boris, he was shouting at someone, then he was fighting again. There was a guy on the ground, in the grass, facedown. Two guys were kicking him. One of the guys kicking was Ronny; he kicked and stomped. It was hard to see through all the people on the porch.

Then a bunch of the fighters were running away. It was the Latino guy and his friends. Ronny and some others ran after them. And then they all disappeared, except Boris and a black guy; they went over and punched and kicked the guy on the ground.

A car drove up very fast. It was a white SUV. There was a person on the hood. The car stopped abruptly and the person fell off into the street. Then the SUV backed up and drove away. Everyone on the lawn ran to the body. I did too. It was Ronny. I could see his face through the heads. His eyes were slightly opened, like a whale's eyes. They lifted him; he was trying to say something. They took him out of the street, and laid him on the grass section between the sidewalk and the street. Then someone yelled. Everyone looked.

The white SUV was driving back. It swerved up onto the sidewalk, toward the group around Ronny. The headlights lit up the whole scene in yellow. Everyone scrambled and dove out of the way, and the SUV drove over Ronny's body. It was fast. His body jerked up from the sidewalk and turned over, so that he was facedown with his arms splayed.

Girls were screaming, and then I knew that it was me who was screaming. I couldn't see anything for a while. The SUV was gone. I walked to the middle of the lawn to see. Boris was at Ronny's side. He was crying. He was trying to turn Ronny over. Everyone was shouting, arguing about what to do. People told Boris not to turn him over. Boris was yelling at everyone to call the police. There was blood coming out on the sidewalk, slowly, from under Ronny's face.

About half of the people walked or ran to their cars and drove off. I saw Katie Hesher crying on the porch with some people comforting her. Some of the neighbors were coming out in sweatpants and slippers. A neighbor woman in a flannel shirt went over to Katie. When I looked back again, the neighbor was kneeling in front of Katie on the steps, comforting her. Boris had turned Ronny over. Ronny's face was smashed on one side, and swollen like a white balloon on the other. Nobody did anything until the police arrived. Boris had his hand on Ronny's chest and was talking softly to him.

There were about five police cars, and then ten, and an ambulance, and a fire truck. All the flashing lights lit up the trees, and they turned the misty rain red, just above the cars.

The paramedics were calm. They checked Ronny, and then gently lifted him onto a gurney and put him into the ambulance.

Then the police were asking for statements. I was one of the people they talked to. A heavy policewoman with regular clothes and brown hair in a bun asked me questions. She had a tough exterior, but she was gentle with me. I told her everything about the car, and about how the fight had started. I told her about when Ronny and I were talking on the couch. She asked if I was Ronny's girlfriend.

I said no.

Did I know him pretty well? No, but.

"But what?" she asked.

"Well, he told me I was smart. I mean, I think he liked me." She looked at me like she didn't understand what I was saying. Then she thanked me, and said she would call if she needed more information.

She never called. The Latino guy, Richard Alvaro, was arrested. Ronny died. I didn't get invited to the funeral. Nobody knew that I was the last person he had talked to.

I worked at Lockheed for the rest of the summer. I didn't draw anymore. My parents could tell I was sad, but I couldn't tell them why. I couldn't even tell Jamie. I didn't do much but watch the moon. It floated there, on the films, reverberant. I began picturing Ronny's face in the moon. My face was there too and he was kissing me. Whenever there was a scratch on the film it would pull me out of the daydream, and I would mark it down.

American History

Then the other day in tenth-grade American History, Mr. Hurston was teaching us about slavery and we had to act out a mock debate between the slave states and the free states. I played Mississippi, and I had to pretend that I wanted slavery to remain legal. Me and the other four slave state guys sat on one side of the room and faced the five kids from the free states. The rest of the class watched us with dull stares.

I'm not the most outgoing person, but no one was really saying anything. So I started it off.

"We need the blacks to be slaves because this country would fall apart without them."

Jerry Holtz represented New York and the good side. Jerry

was handsome and good and a good soccer player. His hair was short in a crew cut and looked just right.

"Look," he said. "We don't want to cause any problems with you slave states, but the country can survive without slavery nowadays. We've established ourselves apart from England, and new industry is taking the country to new levels."

"That may be all fine and dandy for you," I said. I was getting into it a little. "But we Southern states depend on slave labor to run our plantations. It's been done this way since the beginning, and there is no reason to change now."

Then it was funny; something happened. Stephen Gary got really mad.

"What are you people saying?" he said. "It's wrong! It's dead wrong. I can't believe you're talking about it so calmly like this!" Stephen was playing Massachusetts, and he sat next to Jerry. His outburst was a shock to everyone. Stephen's face was flushed, and his eyes were big. He looked mad and like he was going to cry at the same time. Mr. Hurston's face was blank and he stared into the back wall. I looked to the other students. Some were interested in the debate now. Lewis, the only black kid in class, had a blank look on his face too. Stacey, the prettiest girl in class, was picking a scab off the back of her hand.

My slave state partners didn't say anything so I spoke up again.

"It is not wrong," I said to Stephen as calmly as possible. I was being real rational. "It is our God-given right as white Americans to own slaves because we are a superior race."

Stephen's big eyes got bigger, and his mouth became

a black hole. He stood like that and no one said anything. Everyone was waiting. Good Jerry had begun to speak again when Stephen jumped up from his seat, his belly shaking like a water bed. He was screaming.

"You racists! Ray-sists! No wonder Hitler killed all the Jews, because you're all a bunch of racists!"

In general, Stephen was an idiot. He didn't have many friends. He wasn't handsome, he didn't play sports, and he was really quiet. But more than that, he was just strange—the way he picked food from his braces in class and left the little colored bits on his desktop, or like when he told Mrs. Steinbach that he wouldn't read *The Picture of Dorian Gray* because gay people were goblins who stole children to use in sacrifices. But usually he didn't say much.

The class was very interested in the debate now. Ivan and John were laughing silently in the corner. Stacey had stopped picking her scab and looked from Stephen to me.

I said, "I think that that is a pretty racist statement in itself. And I don't really know how it applies, especially because I'm not Jewish, but I think it's the wrong century."

Mr. Hurston broke off his stare and landed back on earth for a second.

"Yes, Stephen, you can't say that because it's a hundred years past the time we're depicting here."

"Hitler is timeless!" screeched Stephen. Now he *was* crying. Most people were laughing out loud now. John and Ivan were about dying in the corner. They slapped each other's back and cackled. Lewis, the black kid, was over in his spot doing nothing.

"Stephen, why don't you sit down," said Mr. Hurston.

"No, I won't sit down! I won't bow down to these racists! They deserve to die! They should burn in the ovens!"

Now even cool Stacey looked surprised. Then she smiled. Everyone was having a great time except Stephen. I really felt bad for him, but Stacey's smile did something to me. If I look back on it, that's what did it, that little upturn at the sides of her glossy pink lips. I wanted to make Stephen go crazy so that I could see Stacey smile.

"Well, Stephen," I said. "Since we're confusing different centuries, why don't I bring up a little book called *The Bell Curve*. It shows that whites and Asians are superior to black people."

"Racist! Racist Jewish institutional testing. It doesn't count," screeched Stephen. He was gesticulating now. His arms swung out at his sides like coiled wet towels and his belly shook some more.

"Boys," said Mr. Hurston. "You can state your opinions as freely as you like, but you must keep the discussion to the 1860s."

Stacey wasn't smiling anymore. She was bored. She went back to picking the scab on the back of her hand.

I should have stopped arguing with Stephen but I didn't. I know I got everything I deserved afterward, but I couldn't stop because I wanted Stacey to laugh. I looked over at Lewis, but he still had that dumb stare. Lewis was a bad student. He hung out with the tough black crowd. There weren't many black students at the school, but a group of them hung out together and acted like they were a gang. Lewis was the runt of the group. It didn't look like anything I was saying even registered with him so I really got into it.

"Niggers," I said, and "Niggers" and "Niggers." I kept saying it as part of my act. And Stephen would scream and bring his arms together in a strangling gesture. He'd grit his teeth and hiss and strangle the air to emphasize his points. I couldn't believe that Mr. Hurston allowed it to go on. It was a real show. Everyone was laughing except Stacey and Lewis.

And then it was over. Mr. Hurston ended the debate a minute before the bell rang. He told Stephen to sit down, but he wouldn't. Then he told the class that it was a great exercise and that it was okay and brave of me to act like I had, using the N word and all, because it gave everyone a sense of what people were like back then.

"Some foolish people have tried to get the N word removed from *Huckleberry Finn* because they find it offensive. Good-intentioned idiots," said Mr. Hurston. "But if they were ever successful, we would lose a sense of what things were like before us. And if we don't know our history . . ."

". . . we're doomed to repeat it," the class mumbled as the bell rang. Everyone stuffed notebooks into bags. From across the room I saw Stephen leave with his head down. Mr. Hurston called after him but he was out the door.

I went back to my regular seat to get my stuff. Stacey's desk was a seat away from mine. She was already packed up when I got there.

"Pretty funny, huh?" I said.

"What?" she asked.

"Stephen, getting all mad like that."

"I thought it was kind of scary," she said. I didn't have anything else to say so she walked out.

The rest of the day was uneventful. I ate lunch, went to the rest of my classes, and then walked home after school. I passed the field and saw Jerry Holtz and the soccer team warming up for the big game against Gunn.

That night I called Stacey. I got her number when I volunteered us for a joint report on the Salem witch trials at the beginning of the year. She never helped me with the report, but I had asked her if I could keep her phone number, just to see how she was doing sometimes. I had never used it.

I was nervous as I called. I had prepared some funny things to say when she answered, but she didn't answer and I didn't leave a message. I called her a few more times that night while I watched *Beavis and Butt-Head* and then *The X-Files*. I got her machine each time. Her voice was hoarse, and the way she said "Stacey" was so raspy and whispered it made me want to squeeze my penis until it hurt. Later, when I called again, I realized that it was a pager, so I typed in my home number. In the middle of playing DOOM on my computer, I heard the phone ring. It was about eleven thirty. There was loud music wherever she was.

"Hello? . . . Hello?" she said, close to the phone. Hearing her voice outside of class made me tingle at the back of my neck.

"Hey, it's Jeremy," I said.

"Oh, hey," she said.

"Where are you?" I asked.

"Hugh?" she said. There were other voices near her.

"What are you doing?" I said.

She was having a hard time hearing me.

"Who is this?"

"It's Jeremy. Jeremy Thompson?"

"Oh, hi. What's up, Jeremy?"

"I don't know . . . I just thought we might hang out some-time."

"Oh. What do you mean?"

"I don't know, I just thought we could maybe do some-thing sometime."

"Okay . . . sure."

"Okay," I said. Then there wasn't much else to say. I forgot all my jokes.

Then she said, "Okay, I'm going to go."

"Okay, I'll call you sometime," I said.

"Okay, bye." She hung up, but not before I heard someone ask, "Who was that?" I bit my lip really hard until it almost bled. Her voice was echoing in the cold air. I was left with my computer screen and the empty room and the blackness outside in the backyard, and everything felt empty. I couldn't go back to my video game with her voice still in my head, and those other voices too. I couldn't play the game anymore without feeling like I was wasting my life. I watched some more television in the living room until my father came home at twelve thirty and told me to go to bed.

I had PE first period. It was a drag getting into those stupid uniforms first thing in the morning. Short green sweat shorts and tight off-white T-shirts. I'd always get depressed playing softball with all the other dweebs who didn't get excused from

PE because they played sports. I'm usually late. The day after Stephen's outburst, I was getting dressed alone in the locker room when Lewis came in, followed by a bunch of the tough black guys: Ezra, Jackson, Damon, Roland, and two big white guys that hung out with them, a fat guy named Mike Farley, and a muscular guy named Damian Petrone. They were all older and all really big. Next to them Lewis was a skinny midget.

Jackson walked up to me. He played running back for the school and got most of our touchdowns. He was six foot three. I was trying to pull on my PE shorts when he pushed me down onto the bench.

"Use that nigger word to my face," he said.

"Excuse me?"

"Come on, use that fucking nigger word to my face, white boy." He put his hand on top of my head so that I couldn't stand up from the bench. He didn't push down; he just held it there so I couldn't stand up.

"Come on, white boy, say that fucking nigger word."

"Call him a nigger," said Mike, the fat white guy.

"Listen, I was just doing it for class, I don't really think those things."

"What things, white boy?" said Jackson.

"Those things I said. I was just saying them because I was supposed to."

"You're supposed to? Your teacher told you to call Lewis a nigger?"

"I didn't call Lewis a nigger."

He slapped me across the face.

"Watch your fucking mouth," he said, not laughing anymore. I looked up at him. I looked at the others. They were all serious now. I turned to skinny Lewis with his big round head.

"Lewis, you know I didn't call you anything."

Lewis didn't say anything. He stood there with his arms crossed. He gave me that same blank stare that he gave me in the classroom.

"Listen, I didn't mean what I was saying, okay? I was just doing it for class and because I wanted to see Stephen Gary get crazy."

"Lewis," said Jackson. That was it, just "Lewis," like they had already talked about doing something and now was the time to do it. Lewis looked at Jackson and then at me, but he just stood there.

In a slow, cold voice Ezra said, "Lewis, break off this motherfucking honky." It came out of his cruel face like a rocky stream.

"Lewis, I was being an idiot. I was just trying to make Stephen crazy. You saw how crazy he got," I said.

"Why'd you want to make him crazy?" said Lewis.

"I don't know. I was just trying to show off. You heard Mr. Hurston, he said I was just doing what I was supposed to do."

Lewis was staring down at me. He didn't look really tough, but he was trying. Then he said, "Thomas Jefferson was doing what he was supposed to do, and he done raped his slaves."

"What?" I said. "What does that mean?"

Lewis stepped back and then hit my nose. There was an explosion between my eyes. I fell back and hit my head against the lockers and fell into the space between the lockers and the bench. My legs were still up on the bench, but my butt was on the cement. I held my nose, and there were tears coming into my eyes, but just as a physical reaction.

I squinted through my fingers and saw Lewis looking down at me. His regular dumb look was angry now. Unsure but trying not to be unsure. I took my hand away from my face and looked at it; there was a lot of blood on my fingers. I heard all the other guys cheering Lewis on. He still looked unsure, but I could tell he was going to do something. I pulled my feet off the bench and slid underneath it. It was really dirty down there and wet. On the underside of the bench there was some old gray gum, and at the bottom of one of the lockers it said I LOVE YOU BITCH! Who wrote that? It was pretty creative.

"Kick that motherfucker!" said the guys.

Lewis stepped back and kicked me. He got me on the top of my head, and he stubbed his toe on my skull, and everyone laughed because he said "Ow, shit" and started dancing around. I lay down there covering my face while they all laughed at Lewis's foot. I waited for more. But it didn't come. The laughter faded, and then they were gone.

For a while I lay on the ground and looked at I LOVE YOU BITCH! Then I got up. I went to the toilet stalls and sat on one of the toilets and waited for the period to end. Just sat there. When the warning bell rang, I stood up and looked at myself in the mirror. My right eye was purple on the inside bottom, and my nose had bled all over my lips and down my neck and onto my off-white PE T-shirt. A nice splatter across the neckline. All the kids were coming in now. Some looked at me, but I didn't wash off and I didn't change my clothes. I left my things in my locker and walked to my next class, American History with Mr. Hurston.

I was there before everyone. I sat at my desk and waited. The middle of my face was throbbing. My classmates started coming in, but no one noticed me. My seat was toward the back. Finally Stacey came in and sat down. She didn't look at me because she never looks at me, but I stared at her really hard until she finally looked.

"Oh my God," she said. "What's wrong with your face?"

"Nothing is wrong with it."

"You're bleeding, Jeremy," she said loudly. "Oh, Jesus, you're *bleeding*!" Other people looked.

"I know," I said. I didn't say anything else; I just stared at her. Real hard.

"Why are you looking at me like that?" she said.

"Because," I said.

"Because what?" She said that quietly, like she was scared.

Then Mr. Hurston came in. He said, "Hello, class, new morning, same old history," like he always did.

"Mr. Hurston," said good Jerry Holtz. "Mr. Hurston, look, Jeremy's bleeding."

"Mr. Hurston, he's staring at me," said Stacey. She was right; I *was* staring at her. Mr. Hurston walked over to my desk. He put his hand under my chin, in the blood, and held my face up to his. I looked into his empty blue eyes. His eyebrows were silvery like his hair.

"What happened?" he asked.

"Nothing," I said.

"Who did this to you?"

"No one."

"Okay, no one did it, right. All right, who?"

"No one."

"Fine, if you won't tell me, I want you to go to the office right now and see Mrs. Moore." He looked around the room. "Jerry, I want you to take Jeremy to the office, to see Mrs. Moore, okay?"

"Sure, Mr. Hurston," said Jerry. He walked to the door and waited for me.

Mr. Hurston let my face go. I didn't stand up yet. I just turned my head and stared at Stacey again.

"What?" she said. She sounded mad now. Everyone was watching.

Then I leaned in and whispered, "I did it for you."

"You did what for me? What are you talking about?"

But I was already standing and walking toward Jerry at the door. There was Lewis walking in with his dumb look.

"Did Thomas Jefferson do that?" I said. And walked past him. I didn't look back, but I could hear people asking Stacey what it was all about.

In the hall Jerry asked me what happened. I told him I was fighting for a girl. He asked who. I told him he wouldn't understand.

"Why did you say you did it for Stacey?" he asked as we crossed the quad toward the tower building.

"What? I didn't."

"I thought you did."

"No."

"Well that's good," he said. "That would have been a shame."

"Why?"

"No, I mean if you had done anything for her." The sun was warm on my back and reflecting off the windows of the office, a bright circle into my eyes.

"I didn't do it for her."

"Cuz she's a total slut," he said.

"I fucking know," I said. But I didn't know. I didn't know anything.

We were almost at the office. The office was an old brick building with a tower in the center with a Spanish cupola. We called it the Tower Building.

As we got closer each window in the tower flashed yellow and white.

At the office Jerry ran up the stairs. He stood at the top and held the door for me. The reflection in the windows above Jerry was as bright as the real sun. As I walked up the steps my face pounded under the skin, I could feel the blood thick and sticky on my clavicle, and I stared right into the burning center of light.

Killing Animals

Birds, and birds, and animals, and things; with slingshots, and BB guns, we killed 'em, and killed 'em. We killed so many.

Every once in a while one of my friends would get a BB gun and we would go on a spree. We'd shoot anything that moved.

When we were in seventh grade, Ronny Feldman and Ami and I slept over at Saul's house. Ronny brought two sling-shots. They were black metal in a scary Y shape; the arms stuck out farther forward than the base. Tied to the arms was plastic tubing that you stretched back, and a soft, greasy little moleskin pad where you put the thing you were firing.

At Saul's we had pepperoni pizza from Domino's and watched *Colors*. We all had three pieces of pizza except Saul—he had five.

Saul was the biggest. He had hair on his belly, balls, and back.

In *Colors,* the Bloods and the Crips were fighting over turf. Blue and red were important to them. The cops were trying to stop the gangs, but the gangs kept fighting. We watched very closely, we couldn't help it.

The movie made me so depressed and I knew the world was ending.

After *Colors,* we watched *Teenage Mutant Ninja Turtles.* It was a movie I liked when I was younger, but after watching *Colors* it was silly. It was silly but I still watched. I tried to forget about the gangs.

Ronny said he liked Michelangelo because he was the funniest.

"I like Michelangelo," he said. "He tells all the jokes." It made sense that Ronny liked Michelangelo because Michelangelo had personality. Ronny himself wasn't very funny, but he was wily.

I liked Michelangelo too, but I was even less funny than Ronny. And I wasn't wily. Leonardo was the leader, Donatello was a scientist, and Raphael was a great fighter. I was none of those.

After the Ninja Turtles, we all arm wrestled on the coffee table. Ronny could beat Ami, and I could beat Ronny. I was surprised, because Ronny was tough even though he was little. It felt good to beat him.

Saul said, "Ryan is stronger than he looks."

Saul could beat everyone at arm wrestling. But it wasn't fair wrestling with him because he was so much bigger. His dick was seven inches. He showed us.

I had no hair under my pits. At the beach, I held my arms down at my sides before I got in the water.

I thought I had no hair because I masturbated so much. But I couldn't stop doing it.

At midnight the house was quiet. We quietly slid open the paneled glass door at the back and left. There was dew on the grass in the backyard, and the air moved slow and cold like a spirit. No one spoke, and it was very quiet. It felt like birth.

We crept to the front yard, and out to the street, and we were away. We were free with the slingshots.

The streets were an empty stage set. All the rules of the daytime were gone.

Each block was lined with gray light posts, with ovate lamps at the top, which cast white-yellow beams onto the cement. The center of the beams, where they hit the pavement, was like nougat.

We passed through the milky light and into the shadows.

Bushes were sentient, and trees shook their leaves in bunches like animals shaking their hides. The wind came in languid gusts like whispered reminders.

We heard cars drive in isolation down Oregon Expressway, in the gray zone, out of sight.

The atmosphere was a held breath, and the shadowed house fronts were sleeping dogs.

*   *   *

We shot rocks at a streetlight two blocks from Saul's house, but the light didn't break. It was made of plastic.

We saw no birds and we wandered.

In front of a low, wide one-story house, a skinny calico cat picked its way on sharp points across the dewy lawn.

"Please don't," I whispered. "Please, please don't."

Ronny lowered his slingshot.

The cat squeezed under a wooden fence. Ronny shot a rock after the cat, but it just hit the fence.

I was happy for the cat, but I suddenly felt very lonely.

Farmers, Italians, and sociopaths kill cats. Sociopaths piss in their beds. French people use piss as perfume.

I had a black and white cat named Toby. When he was young, the neighbor cut his balls off for eating fish from his pond. I wasn't born when that happened.

We walked across town and ended up at Mitchell Park.

Mitchell Park was big, with baseball fields, and soccer fields, and playgrounds, and a pool. Next door was our junior high school, J.L.S. J.L.S. was far from all our houses because it was the only junior high in the city.

I used to play soccer at Mitchell Park when I was younger. When I was ten, my team, the Blue Scorpions, got into the intercounty championship. The playoffs were at Mitchell Park. We won and won, and got to the finals. I played defense and defended a lot.

My dad yelled like crazy until one game the ref told him to leave.

In the finals we played an East Palo Alto team, the Red Bullets. They were all black kids and we were all white. They were all bigger than we were. They just kept getting by me.

At night the park was empty. There was nothing to shoot, so we wandered around the dark park. We walked through the playground. There were some animals on springs that little kids could ride. A horse and a seal and a lion. We kicked them until the lion lost his face; it was bent inward, the eyes all wrong.

There was a municipal shed in the middle of the park. Saul and Ronny and Ami boosted me up to a transom that was cracked open. I pulled the transom open and scrambled through like a squirrel. I dropped down into the dark and then opened the door from the inside.

There was nothing in there but a bunch of basketballs, and footballs, and soccer balls, and cones, and stuff like that. We took the balls out and threw them into the air and shot them, but they didn't pop. Then we kicked them all over.

We walked across the park and went to our school. It was called J.L.S. after J. L. Stanford, the guy who built the university. At night the hallways were dark, and the walls were gray and grim.

We shot pellets through the windows. The pellets made little mosquito bites in the glass. We would be able to admire our work on Monday.

We carved with rocks into the window of Mr. Shepard's Social Studies classroom. I wrote FUCK HOMER because we were learning about the Greeks. Ronny carved a swastika. We

43

all told him he was stupid. Saul and Ami were both Jewish, and so was I, but I wasn't raised Jewish.

Ronny just thought the swastika was funny.

We kicked over some trash cans, and then walked back toward Saul's along Middlefield Road.

We passed Simone Chris's house. She had been my girl-friend in fourth grade. I fought Sam Tuttle for her. He was tall and thin like a scarecrow, and said that he liked her. One lunch, everyone gathered behind the elementary school library, and Sam and I got ready to fight. I kicked Sam in the shin and he fell to the ground holding his leg. I felt awesome.

But I got in trouble, especially because I took karate at the YMCA, and karate was supposed to be for self-defense.

Then Simone broke my heart. She left me for Rio Gereaux, a gymnast. It was fourth grade, but it was still a big deal. I mean, when are things supposed to start mattering? Now, and now, and now.

Before we hit Loma Verde, we passed Unity church. It was where my mom took me when I was little. She was Jewish, but she went to church because she liked the minister, a smiley guy named Stan.

One time at Sunday school I won a Bible in a raffle. It had all of Jesus's words written in red. Fish, and loaves, and the first will be last, and thy neighbor, and Caesar, and an eye for a tooth, and he killed the fig tree because it wouldn't give him fruit.

We shot BBs at the Unity church. The BBs made little pop-ping sounds when they went through the church windows. Seeing those little vein-filled bites used to scare me when I was younger. They made me think of anonymous bad people with destructive things in their hands. Faceless and swirling. Now we were the bad people.

We stopped by 7-Eleven and bought some Hostess apple pies. They came in a bright green rectangular wrapper. I paid for Ronny's. He got cherry flavor and it came in a red wrapper.

Two cops came in as we were walking out. A skinny, young white cop and a fatter, older black cop. They were talking about something. We were twelve years old and it was two a.m. Ronny and Saul had the slingshots in the backs of their pants, under their shirts. The cops didn't even look at us as we passed.

After we walked out, I looked back. Inside, the cops were buying coffee and laughing. I could see the steam rising from the cups on the counter before they put the lids on.

We walked back to Saul's eating our pies. They were crescent shaped and glazed. We took big bites and they were very sweet, and we all wanted some milk but we didn't have any.

A week later the four of us went out with the slingshots during the day. We went to Greer Park, near the 101 freeway. Across the freeway was East Palo Alto.

There were tons of birds in Greer, but we had to be discreet because there were adults with children around.

We traded off with the slingshots, and shot metal pellets and rocks at the birds in the trees. We were bad shots; we hit nothing.

One bird flew away, and Ronny tried to shoot it as it flew. He aimed too low, and the pellet went across the street, into the window of a ground-floor apartment. We ran.

We looked back and a black man was running after us. He was lithe, and serious, and fast. There was no way to get away so we stopped when he was close.

We told him we were just trying to hit birds.

The man didn't look so mad then.

"Oh," he said. "Okay. I just have a baby in the house, and it usually sits in its cradle right under that window you shot. She wasn't there, but, you know, I just can't have broken glass fall on her."

We told him that we understood.

Then he let us go.

When we were almost back at Saul's house, we saw a dove sitting in a tree. While he was still walking, Saul shot a pellet at it and hit it. It fell like a heavy glove, and hit the cement with a dull sound. We walked over. Its round, black eye was open and looking up at the sky. The pellet was in the back of its head and there was a little blood in its smooth feathers.

At the end of the year, we all went to Ami's bar mitzvah. We weren't all friends anymore, but we were still nice to one another. At the party I arm wrestled Ronny again, and I could still beat him.

In eighth grade I went to a new school. Jordan Middle School reopened because there were so many kids in Palo Alto. More kids than in the old generation.

Jordan's old mascot was a dolphin, but we voted and

changed the mascot to a jaguar. A dolphin was stupid because there was no ocean around.

But there were no jaguars or jungles around either.

But one time there was a mountain lion that wandered through Palo Alto. It had come down from the hills above Stanford. Eventually it climbed a tree above Juana Briones Elementary School. They shot it so that it wouldn't eat the kids.

Ronny and Saul stayed at J.L.S. and Ami had different friends, so I made new friends at Jordan. My new friends were Ed and Ivan. Neither of them was handsome.

After school, the three of us would go to Ed's and sit in his room and listen to Guns N' Roses' *Use Your Illusion* and *The Best of Bob Dylan,* and *The Best of Jimi Hendrix,* and *The Best of the Doors.* Ed's house was near the school, and we would go there and make Campbell's soup on the stove, and I would put in lots of extra spices like oregano. Ed said that I put in too many, but I liked all the spices.

Sometimes we would smoke tobacco out of the meerschaum pipe Ed's dad gave him. Sometimes we would take his dad's liquor from the cabinet. When we took some, we'd put water back in the bottles so his dad wouldn't know.

We were also friends with Dan and Jerry, but they were jocks and were different. They were more popular with the girls, but sometimes they spent time with us, especially when we were drinking.

We also hung out with Howard Vern. He was anorexic, the only anorexic boy I have heard of. He had an awful body shaped like a pear, with skinny arms and skinny legs, and cellulite on his stomach. We said he was "skinny-fat."

One time, Ed and Ivan and Howard, and I went over to Ed's after school. Howard brought a water balloon launcher. Ed's parents weren't at home so we drank some Jim Beam, and then we picked a bunch of fat oranges from the tree in Ed's backyard, and went up on the roof with the water balloon launcher.

When kids rode by on their bikes, we shot oranges at them. Girls and boys.

The launcher launched the oranges hard. It must have hurt when they hit. Tom Prince rode by and we hit him right on his big ass. It sounded like a slap on a face, and even from the roof, I could see his ass ripple through his pants. He got off his bike and started throwing oranges back at us on the roof.

Tom Prince had horrible face acne, which sprouted in small groupings, like piles of bat shit. The piles were always runny because he would pick at them. He was an angry, fat young man.

He threw a bunch of oranges, but he couldn't hit us. We laughed and laughed at the fat-ass on the ground.

Howard was laughing too.

Then Tom stopped throwing and yelled, "What the fuck are you laughing at, you anorexic fuck? Why don't you go and slit your wrists again, you fat, pear-shaped piece of shit."

Howard stopped laughing. He yelled at Tom so loudly he almost fell off the roof. It was funny that Tom called Howard a pear, because Tom was shaped like a pear too. An even fatter pear than Howard. Tom got on his bike and rode off and Howard was still yelling.

We shot at more kids with the launcher. Then we hit a

48

small Asian girl in the head and it made her fall off her bike. We hid on the back side of the roof and peeked over. She was crying when she picked up her bike. But she didn't do anything; she just got back on and rode off.

When I left Ed's that evening to go home, the street was strewn with smashed oranges.

When I got home, my cat, Toby, was waiting for me.

On weekends we had nothing to do. The girls didn't like us like they liked Jerry and Dan. When they didn't have plans with the girls, Jerry and Dan would hang out with us. We would go out egging.

We would go out on a weekend night at about nine and ride our bikes to the Lucky's supermarket on Alma. Late at night there was hardly anyone in the store, and the checkout clerk didn't care that we were buying five dozen eggs. "Making some omelets," we would say. Sometimes we would go next door to Bob's Donuts and buy some bear claws and milk.

Then we would ride around and look for late-night joggers and walkers. If we saw a couple taking a stroll, we would pelt the shit out of them. Usually the man would have to get macho and chase us, but they never caught us. Except Howard. Howard was always the slowest, and he would get caught and have to cry his way out of a fight.

One time Ivan and I stole a motorized scooter. It was sitting in an open garage and we walked in and took it. We could fit two on it: one to drive and one to throw eggs. It was tiny, but it went pretty fast.

Ivan and I were out on the scooter one night. We didn't have money to buy eggs, so we took some hard-boiled eggs from my fridge. We saw a white guy in a leather jacket walking with an Asian woman. Ivan slowed down, and I hit the man with two hard-boiled eggs, right on his jacket. I hit the girl once in the head and she bent over. Three hits was pretty good shooting.

The man chased us, but we were long gone.

We went to 7-Eleven to play Street Fighter II. Ivan was better at it. He could play with Ryu, Zangief, Dhalsim, or Blanka. Zangief was Russian like Ivan, but Ivan reminded me more of Blanka. Blanka was a Brazilian beast of some sort. Ivan was kind of a beast. Like he was mean on the outside and sensitive on the inside. And Blanka means "white" in Spanish, and Ivan was very pale, so it all just made me think of him.

I could only play with Guile, a U.S. military guy who could do back flips. But he had a special invisible throw if you knew the code.

In the middle of one of our games, a car pulled up in the parking lot.

I just knew.

"Run," I said to Ivan. I ran out the door just as the man in the leather jacket got out of the car.

Across the parking lot, I looked back and saw Ivan messing with the scooter. The man in the leather jacket grabbed him and put him on the ground, and then started kicking him. I stopped running, but I didn't go back. I just watched.

The Asian woman was in the front seat of the car. She looked over at me. She didn't look sad for Ivan at all. When she started calling to the man in the leather jacket, I ran.

I saw Ivan at school on Monday. He had a black eye and his bottom lip was purple at the side. We never talked about the man with the leather jacket to each other, but Ivan told people about it. Ivan told the story like I had left 7-Eleven before the guy even came.

Brian was a kid from Los Angeles. He had a tattoo of an eight ball on his leg, but it was smeared. He wasn't supposed to get it wet the day after he got it, but he took a shower. It looked like a drawing that had been wiped with a sponge.

I went with him to JJ's house. JJ was a skateboarder. He had a half-pipe in his backyard. I wasn't good on the half-pipe.

JJ had a BB gun. We stood in his backyard and shot at birds that flew overhead, but didn't hit any.

JJ sold me the BB gun for $50.

When I had the BB gun, Ivan and Ed and Dan and Jerry and I took it out. We walked in the creek by my house, Matadero. It was a cement creek that ran from one side of town to the other. The water got really high when it rained. My dad said not to go in it. He said that every winter, when the water got high, kids would take a raft in it, and someone would drown.

But that was when I was little. When I was in eighth grade, we went into it all the time. Sometimes we would catch crawfish and step on them and they'd crunch. We also burned things down there: a stuffed bear that an ugly girl gave me on Valentine's Day, sitting on a little wooden chair that my brother made. It smelled like chemicals.

We walked down the creek with a BB gun. Dan hit a bird, and it dropped to the dirt. It wasn't dead, so he shot it a bunch more times until it stopped moving.

We shot at house windows from the creek. We made designs in the glass. We almost made a smiley face in one, but the eyes were crooked.

We walked down the creek, all the way to Hoover Park. Some men were working on a roof. They were bent over in construction hats and hammering boards. Jerry aimed at one of the men. He missed once, and then he hit him. The man stood up. The way he stood, we knew Jerry got him in the ass. The man looked around and then he ran to the side of the roof. We all ran back down the creek toward my house.

It was far to get back to my house. In the bottom of the cement creek the water was low and we ran down there. The bottom was covered in slime and it was easy to slip, but it was harder to see us down there because the cement walls on the sides were high.

We could see the construction man's car stop on all the bridges over the creek. He was looking for us, and we ran faster.

Finally we made it back to my house.

Inside, we rested. We watched some of *Diff'rent Strokes,* and then everybody left.

Later, someone stole the BB gun. I don't know who, but they're out there shooting things.

*   *   *

In high school, Howard Vern got a paint pellet gun. The balls were brightly colored: yellow, green, red, blue, white, orange, and black. They were round and waxy like candy.

One night I slept over at Howard's house. At midnight, Bill came by in his jeep. Bill was handsome, but retarded. It was hard for him to put sentences together, and his emotions were all fucked-up. Other days, he and I spent a lot of time smoking pot and doing pull-ups on a bar above his bedroom door.

I wasn't friends with Jerry or Dan anymore. They played on the school sports teams, and started calling me a fag after I quit the football team. They said Ed and I were gay together. It made me want to stay away from Ed because everyone started saying we were gay. Some girls even made up a song and a dance about us. I never saw the dance, but I heard about it.

Bill and Howard and I drove around town thinking about things to shoot with the paint pellet gun. We shot stop signs and mailboxes, and we shot at the high school, but those things weren't very fun.

"Let's go shoot Alice Henderson's house," I said.

Alice was the girl who made up the gay dance about me. I think that she was mad at me, and at everyone because she was a slut, and everyone knew that she was a slut. I guess the song and dance helped her anger out.

Howard and Bill thought Alice Henderson's was a great idea and we drove over to the richest part of town, at the end of University Avenue.

All the houses were very big in the area, but Alice's was

one of the biggest. Bill pulled up and I leaned out the back-door window and fired. The pellets hit the house with a hard, wet sound. I spread the shots around the front of the house, and they left dark flowers on the side of the white wall. I kept thinking of the words *crime, crime, crime,* and *faggot, faggot, faggot.*

I was a dark agent of the night, delivering terror in the suburbs while the inhabitants slept. I was evil in anyone's eyes, but in high school, underhanded action rules.

After Alice's we wanted more so we shot some other houses. We shot Jerry's house because he ditched me as a friend, and Eli Fox's house because he was an annoying guy Howard knew from Hebrew school, and Anna Zimmerman's house because she had a big crush on me and had no chin. She had given me the bear that we burned.

Later we got caught because Howard's mom found paint on his clothes. She was a friend of Eli Fox's parents. The Foxes turned us in and we had to do community service. Jerry called me a fag to my face in front of everyone at school, but he was too scared to start a fight. And I heard that Alice kept doing the gay dance about me.

Some people when they were young shot deer, and foxes. Faulkner shot a bear, Hemingway shot lions and a lot of things. Gangs shoot people for initiation.

We shot animals, and people. But they were all small animals, and we didn't kill anyone.

Emily

He was so cute. Younger, but I didn't care. He was a change from the assholes in my grade like Adam and Roberto who just wanted to fuck and do it in the ass. Or come on my face like a porn, and tell their friends about it. And with them I was always the last call.

The first time I saw Ryan was over at the Oldses' house, John and Steve's. Everyone would go over there all the time. John with all the sophomores and Steve with all the juniors. It was the hangout house. I was always there because Maddy Patten was going out with Steve.

Ryan was there one day. It was after school. He was in John's room, sitting on the edge of the bed playing a video game. He had a black Yankees hat on and he looked like an angel. I could tell that he was different, sweeter than the others. He had pain in his eyes.

I stared at him without him knowing. Or maybe he knew. I came up with all these fantasies just watching him play the video game. I didn't talk to him then.

Two weeks later, there was a party at the Patten twins' house. They're my best friends, Elsie and Maddy. The boys called Elsie "Last-Call" because her name sounded like "L-C." Maddy was still with Steve.

At the party, we three were playing I Never with a bunch of other girls. Someone says, "I never . . . ," and if you've done the thing that they say, like cheated on a boyfriend, you have to drink.

"I never had sex at school."

I drank.

"I never had sex with two guys at once."

I drank.

"I never had sex with three guys at once."

When it was my turn to say "I never," I had a hard time thinking of things to say. I said, "I've never been in love." So stupid.

A couple of the girls drank. Elsie didn't drink, but Maddy did, and I thought she was stupid because that meant that she loved Steve. But then I thought that maybe it wasn't so stupid. There was something inside me that was saying that I was in love with Ryan, even though I had never talked to him. I had this feeling all of a sudden like I wanted to take care of him.

Then it was funny because he walked in. He was with John Olds and some sophomores. I stopped playing I Never and I went over to him.

"Hey," I said.

His friends gave him looks. He acted shy. He was like a deer.

"Hey," he said.

"You wanna play quarters?"

He and his friends and me and some junior girls played. Pork, and Adi, and the Pattens, and me versus the sophomore boys.

We were playing on the island in the kitchen. I'm very good at quarters. They were very bad, and we killed them. After a while they all looked sick. We played eight rounds and they got it in once. On the eighth round, Ryan's friends each took a tiny sip because they couldn't take anymore. They left the whole pitcher for Ryan.

"You gotta drink it all, shithead," said Pork. She *was* a porker. All the guys called her Pork because she had big tits and a big ass, she was loud and rude, and her hair was big and brown and curly like a beast's. I told her to shut up. Ryan took the pitcher in both hands and drank. It started spilling around the sides of his mouth and onto his shirt. He got wet and then wetter. He couldn't finish it all.

"Finish the backwash," said Pork.

"Shut up, Pork," I said.

I never called her Pork to her face. Elsie laughed.

"Fuck you, bitch, go ahead and play with your little kids,"

said Pork, and she left the kitchen. I laughed. Elsie said she was going to piss, and the other girls left. Ryan was trying to take big breaths, but he was doing it very slowly. He was swaying.

"Do you need some air?" I asked.

I took him to the backyard, but a bunch of the junior and senior guys were out there. We went around to the side of the house, to a little side yard. Above, there was a trellis with jacaranda flowers; underneath it was dark and cool. He put one hand on the fence and hung his head. He breathed slowly. Then he crouched low to the ground. He threw up against the fence. I laughed a little, but only to myself. I put my hand gently on the top of his head. After he was done I helped him up under his arm. We stood for a minute in the cool dark. He was hunched with his hands on his thighs. We said nothing, but it was like we were talking. Finally, I asked if he wanted some water.

We were back in the kitchen, and I got a glass from the cupboard and took some water from the sink. He took a sip. Then he took another one. Through the kitchen door I could see Pork talking to Adam and some other guys. They were looking toward me and laughing. Adam made a gesture and smiled. I turned back to Ryan.

"You feel better?"

He nodded. He did look a little better. He finished the water. I took the glass and put it in the sink.

"Follow me," I said. I took his hand. We went upstairs. I led him down the hall to the twins' parents' room. He didn't say anything. I told him to sit on the side of the bed. I told him to lie back and he did. His feet were on the floor. Then I undid his pants. I pulled his boxer shorts down to his feet. I did it for a while. He made sounds.

I stopped. I said, "Do you want to do anything else?"

He said, "No."

After it was finished, he pulled his pants back up. I sat on the side of the bed next to him. I asked him if he liked it.

We went downstairs. At the bottom of the stairs I stopped and he kept walking. The party was dying, but there were still people there. These people seemed slow and drunk and smiley and evil. I went into the kitchen to get some water. I went to the sink and picked up the glass Ryan used before. There was some water in it and someone had put a cigarette in it. I cupped my hands and drank right from the faucet. I turned off the water and walked out toward the living room, where I had seen Adam before. Now Ryan was sitting on the couch with Adam. Adam was laughing. Ryan was laughing too in a shy way.

When Stacey died no one knew what happened. It was after the homecoming dance. *Of course* Stacey was sophomore princess. She was that kind of person. A cheerleader. She was going out with Casey McDonald, and it was weird because it seemed like Casey really liked her. They were going out for six months. I saw them over the summer, at Steve Olds's, and one time at Lake Tahoe during the Fourth of July. It was crazy. We were at a huge party. One thousand people at one house. Tosh Masuda was there with Adam and all those guys.

Tosh had a gun, and when the fireworks started going off, Tosh started shooting the gun in the air. It was really stupid; the bullets could have fallen back and hit someone.

And Casey and Stacey were there, and it was so weird because Casey actually looked happy. Before Stacey, he hated girls. He and Byron would just fuck them and treat them like shit. He was in Roberto's club, the Dirty Dozen. They all competed to see who could fuck the most girls. Sometimes they videotaped it.

But there he was, with Stacey, watching the fireworks. Both were holding red keg cups, and they had big smiles on their faces, even when Tosh was shooting the gun. And I had never had that. I had never had a boyfriend. I had never watched fireworks with anyone.

Homecoming was just like every other dance, it wasn't a big event. We weren't in Texas. The twins and I got pretty drunk and we stood in the corner of the gym and snuck apricot schnapps from my purse and laughed at the idiots. I didn't see Ryan. I wanted to call him but I didn't have his number. I saw John Olds and I asked him where Ryan was. He said that Ryan was out of town for the weekend.

After that I wanted to leave. The ceremony was going on. Stacey was up there with the other princesses. Then they had the Royal Court Dance. Stacey ditched her sophomore prince and danced with Casey. His eyes were closed and her eyes were closed. I guess it was their last dance. Guns N' Roses were playing.

I went outside to have a cigarette. Adam was out there smoking. He was drunk. He told me to follow him, and we went to the pool. We walked to the place in the fence behind the diving boards where the barbed wire is fucked up. He climbed the fence and jumped over.

He told me to climb over. I threw my purse to him and I climbed, but it was harder than I thought. My heels kept getting caught. I should have taken them off. When I got over I was tired.

He wanted to get into the pool and I said no. He took his clothes off. He had a swimmer's body. He was very good-looking. Like an Israeli hero. Freshman year he was too pretty; he looked like a girl. Then he became a man.

He jumped in the pool and he was in the pool, swimming around naked.

"Get in the pool, Emily."

"No."

"Get in the fucking pool."

"No."

Another night I would have, but it didn't seem fun that night. It was old and familiar. Adam was mad because he could tell I was changing.

"You can be a real cunt, you know that?"

He was swimming toward the side of the pool like a shark. I started backing away. He got out, naked; I knew he was going to throw me in, and I had my dress on. I ran but I was in my heels. At the fence, I looked back and he was coming, his dick was flapping. I tried to climb, but he grabbed me off the fence. I screamed. He carried me over his shoulder. I scratched his back and bit his shoulder. He kept walking, and then threw me in.

Once I was in, he started putting his clothes back on. I was yelling at him and trying to splash him so that his clothes would be wet too, but I didn't get him. My dress came up around me like a silver-pink jellyfish.

When he was dressed, he climbed the fence and left. I floated for a while in the black water and then I climbed out. My purse was by the fence. I picked it up and took out a cigarette and sat at the edge of the pool and let my legs dangle in the water with my heels on.

There was a moon and it was on the water. A miniature moon rocking on the little waves. I always see nice images like that but I don't know what to do with them. I guess you share them with someone. Or you write them down in a poem. I had so many of those little images, but I never shared them or wrote any of them down.

I smoked the whole cigarette and then flicked it into the pool. I lit another one and stood up in my wet dress and walked to the fence. I took a drink of apricot schnapps. I took my heels off and threw them over the fence. I climbed and this time the fence hurt my toes and feet. I picked up my shoes and went back to the dance, dripping water as I went.

The two mothers at the door gave me a funny look, but I walked past before they could say anything. Inside, everyone was dancing to Dr. Dre. I saw Adam on the other side of the gym with Byron and Roberto. Adam's hair was still wet and slicked back. They were laughing. I walked around and walked up behind Adam and I poured my apricot schnapps over his head.

Roberto made a noise like "Ooooooooo." All the schnapps

hadn't come out before Adam turned around, so I started flinging it in his face. He tried to grab my arms. He grabbed the left one, the one without the bottle. I kept splashing it in his face and he couldn't get my right arm to make me stop. Roberto was laughing a lot in the background, and everyone around made a circle because I was yelling and calling Adam a Jew motherfucker. Finally he slapped me across the face. I swung the bottle and it hit him above his eye. Then I dropped the bottle and it broke on the floor.

That was when Mr. Forest, the dean, tried to break it up, but Adam had already grabbed me. He threw me on the gym floor. There was a squeaking sound, like basketball shoes during a game.

They sat us in the medic's room, where the athletes usually go, and called our parents, but my mom didn't answer. They kept me there until she answered. One hour later she answered and then she came and they told her what happened. We drove home and my mom wasn't very mad at me.

Later at home, my mom and I were smoking cigarettes at the kitchen table. All the lights were out except for the one in our little kitchen nook. The place was filled with smoke. Then the phone rang. For a second I thought about Ryan, but my mom said it was Adam. I walked over and hung it up.

"You don't want to talk to him?"

"He's an asshole, they all are."

"Are you going to break up?"

"He's not my boyfriend!"

We sat and smoked. It was dark except for the overhead light, which was brown-yellow. Everything seemed yellow: the fridge, the kitchen table. The living room rug was a dirty yellow. My mom's face, and the camel on the box. I saw me and my mom from outside my head. Two yellow-haired women sitting across a yellow table in a yellow kitchen full of smoke.

My mom went to bed and I smoked some more cigarettes.

A while later there was a tapping at the door. At first I didn't think about it because it was really soft, but it was constant and regular so I became aware of it.

I knew it was Adam. I sat at the table and it kept going, soft and steady. The door was in the darkness outside the circle of light in the kitchen. God, I didn't want to open it.

It felt like I could sit there forever, and the tapping would never stop.

Camp

We all went to the camp.

We were twelve and thirteen years old. Me and Ivan and Howard and Ute and Ed. Jewish, Russian, Jewish, Italian, and half Korean/half white. I had turned thirteen in April.

It was a YMCA water-ski camp. There was a husband and wife who ran everything, but the husband was the head counselor. The husband had well-manicured dark hair and a clipped beard that fit his face; the wife had blond hair to her shoulders. He was in his forties and she looked younger. A pleasant, Christian-looking mom and dad.

He wore a tan explorer's hat with a floppy brim and a string that hung down under his chin. His wife did the roll call and made sure everybody was where they should be. They both led the songs around the campfire at night, but she led more of them. Sometimes he would play his guitar. We sang many different songs, and sometimes the husband told ghost stories. It sounded like he had told the stories a million times, but that he was trying to make them exciting each time. I think he was very proud of them and thought they were good just because he had told them so many times. At the end we always sang "The Lion Sleeps Tonight."

It was so dirty around the fire and I'd always get smoke in my mouth.

We were too old for the camp.

Jane was our counselor even though we were all boys. She was the daughter of the head counselor and his wife. Jane had blond hair like her mom. Later she told us that she was the black sheep of her family.

Another counselor was Hulk.

Hulk was very tall and big, like a bulky potato shape, fat but really strong. He had huge calves that were red from the sun because he wore shorts all the time. His shorts hung to his fat knees and he had them in all ugly colors, like pink, and they were dirty and worn from the woods. Or fluorescent orange with swirl designs, or cut-off denim. He wore big brown Timberland boots without tying the laces. He had a curly mullet and a goatee and he wore Vuarnet sunglasses. The Vuarnets were a single lens that went across both eyes and reflected rainbows in the sunlight.

Ed and I had had him for a counselor the first time, when

we were eight. That was for a different camp in a different set of woods, but Hulk was the same then.

Howard was Jewish and I was Jewish because my mom was Jewish. I never went to Hebrew school but I was circumcised.

When I was a kid my friend Nick and I made a potion together. Nick was French; his dad had a pointy beard and spoke with an accent. We got a big rectangular plastic tub and put snails in it and red pyracantha berries, which were poisonous and made the blackbirds drunk so they flew into the windows and died. And we took cat poo from the sandbox with a plastic shovel and put it in the soup. At the end we peed in it. My penis was like a mushroom and my French friend's was draped in skin, like a monk's cowl.

We tried to get my little brother to drink it but he wouldn't. We left our potion in the backyard in the rectangular tub. One day I found a dead rat next to it.

In fourth grade Mr. DeFelice was my teacher. He was younger than all the other teachers. He said his name meant he was always happy. He told us he ate pizza and drank beer at Luigi's in Mountain View. That was the next city over, but far for me. He said he was good at Top Gun on Nintendo. He could get to the space level. A jet in space doesn't make sense.

* * *

In ninth grade we watched a lot of Holocaust stuff. We saw pictures and then a film of the naked bodies being bulldozed. Penises on the men and vaginas and breasts on the women. They didn't seem like real penises. I looked close. Some were big.

I had a cat named Toby. He was put to sleep at the vet's. Gassed? Buried? Incinerated. Way of all flesh and fur.

Ed was at my very first Y camp when we were eight. He was half Korean from his mom, and his dad was a big, white, bald dork. One morning Hulk took us to the lake. It was so cold. We had our towels around our shoulders. Mine was *The Incredible Hulk,* Ed had *The Dukes of Hazard.* There was a Confederate flag on the side of their car.

Hulk said we were all in the Polar Bear Club. He was the whale of the club.

We took our shirts off. Nobody had muscles. Hulk said he would give a Coke to whoever went in the lake naked.

One night in ninth grade we were drunk and wandering around the neighborhoods in a pack. There were some girls with us too. There was nowhere to go and no more alcohol.

We walked through Mid-Peninsula, the school for bad kids who got kicked out of other schools. They were allowed to smoke cigarettes during their brunch break. They were mostly white and they wore a lot of black. One year a kid brought a gun to school and shot his ex-girlfriend at brunch because she had a new boyfriend. Then he shot the new boyfriend. Then he shot himself. The girl didn't live, but the new boyfriend lived.

We never had any black friends. Not before high school and not in high school. But we liked black rappers. Dr. Dre, 2Pac, DJ Quik, Too $hort, and the Geto Boys.

At water-ski camp there was a black girl, Angela. She had no friends at camp because she was weird. She would talk about aliens. She said she and her brothers saw aliens, but it sounded like her brothers were her only friends and that her brothers were the ones who came up with the alien idea.

We dared Howard to make out with her in the back of the bus. He did one night. On the way back to the campsite he kissed her, but it was messy, like two lizards. We were in the seat in front of them and we saw him feel her small breasts, and under the towel he felt her vagina. We looked back and saw it all. It was a purple towel with nothing on it. He was the first of us to do all that, but it was with the black alien girl.

I had my first girlfriend in fourth grade, in Mr. DeFelice's class. Her name was Simone. She was pretty and blond like Madonna. After she broke up with me I would watch *Who's That Girl?* to remind myself of her. Once Simone said Mr.

DeFelice asked if he could take pictures of her at his house, but her mom wouldn't let her go.

Ute's name was the name of an Indian tribe. He was Italian but his parents were hippies and accountants at Whole Foods. His older brother was named Rain, he was two years older than us. Rain had the biggest dick of all his friends. He would walk around naked and show it, all his friends talked about it. They called him "Calcium."

Calcium broke all the basketball records in high school and had sex with tons of ugly girls.

Later, in high school, Ute had sex first out of all of us. It was with a black girl, Venus.

I had sex last. I was drunk at a party at my friend Barry's house. We did it in a bedroom, Susan and me, and then stayed the night. In the morning, I waited till she left, and then I walked home alone.

At water-ski camp we told everyone about Howard and the black girl on the bus. There was a handsome guy, Chad. He got into a fight with Howard and punched him in the eye. Chad didn't get in trouble because he told the counselors about what Howard did to Angela.

* * *

After I had sex once I had sex a lot. The second time was in Susan's bed. I was about to come and I pressed my foot against the footboard. My long toenails scraped against the board like cockroaches. After, when we pulled away, it was sticky and frothy. Buttery, like pulling apart a Baby Ruth.

She rolled over and cried.

When I was eight, we all loved Coke. The bright red can with the cold brown liquid. There was one machine back at the main counselor's cabin. If we did something good we got a can.

Everybody in the Polar Bear Club wanted a Coke. But no one wanted to get naked in front of Hulk. Hulk took his shirt off. He was fat and pale and had hair on the front of his shoulders. His stomach was like curdled milk. There were little chunks of ill-formed fat that showed through the skin when he moved. The skin on his stomach was as white as the inside of a radish.

In fourth grade, in Mr. DeFelice's class, I had to sit next to Sasha Alexander. She wore the thickest glasses I've ever seen. She had short red hair, lots of freckles, and no friends.

The class practiced writing cursive. We had to write our desk partner's name. Mr. DeFelice came around to inspect. He told me my *x* in *Alexander* looked like a swastika.

*   *   *

In eleventh grade we studied the Civil War. There were the Bad Confederates and the Good Guys in the North. Some people still believe that the Confederates were right.

The water-ski camp went to Knott's Berry Farm. Ute and Howard and I and the others weren't allowed to go into Knott's Berry Farm because of the fight Howard had with Chad and because of what Howard did with the black girl and because he told that we had made him do it. The head counselor and his wife wanted to kick us out of camp, but instead we missed out on Knott's Berry Farm. It was Hulk's idea. We stayed in the parking lot by the bus with Jane and threw a Frisbee. Jane had to stay because she was our counselor. She was sad for us. That was when she told us that she was the black sheep of the family.

At the very end of the day we got to go into Knott's Berry Farm. We saw Chad. He had his T and C tank top on. He had met a local girl in the park. His friend told us that Chad had got to second base with her already when they went on the mine ride. She was blond and pretty.

Riding back to the campsite, Ute drew pictures of people being burned in ovens. He burned Howard and Chad and Hulk in his ovens. They went in as they were—it looked like them, Ute was good at drawing cartoons—and they came out as skeletons.

A little kid told about the drawings. Hulk came back and saw the pictures. Back at camp he told us how bad the Nazis were and that it was not something to joke about.

Nobody in the camp liked us.

*   *   *

Ute was handsome but he was a nerd too. He drew lots of pictures. Ed and I drew pictures with him. We made our own comic called *The Alien Brothers*. We drew ourselves like vicious aliens and killed the people in our school.

In fourth grade Sasha Alexander was the biggest dork I could ever think of. Buckteeth and short red hair and glasses. She said she could play basketball better than me. I laughed. We played at lunch and I won. She didn't admit that I won. Back in class I told her she was a dork and a poor loser, and she stabbed me in the arm with a pencil. The hole was gray from the graphite.

    Mr. DeFelice didn't do anything about it.

When we were eight this guy pulled Ed's bathing suit off. Ed didn't have a mushroom. He was half Korean. We were scared to fight the big guy who did it. Hulk didn't know about it, so the kid didn't get in trouble.

In high school it was mostly white kids. There were only about thirty black students. Some were bussed in from East Palo Alto. Most of them hung out in an area in front of the school library. That was their spot. They got bad grades and wore parkas.

*   *   *

That night at Mid-Pen we were drunk and tired of walking. Me and Ivan and Ed and Jack stood on the cement-filled tire of a tetherball pole. We held the pole and rocked the tire back and forth and sang drunken songs. The rest of the group left.

We were drunk and we came up with our own songs. We sang about Heebs, and stingy Jews. Not meanly, just loud and funny. I sang loud.

Ute was mad about it, he asked how we could do that to Dave Frankel and Howard, and he left. No one cared. We didn't care about Howard, he was a fool.

At water-ski camp we made fun of Howard and the black girl, Angela, so much. Late at night we snuck out of our sleeping bags and smoked pot. At campfire one night we dared Howard to push Angela in the water.

We sang "Wimoweh, wimoweh," and then as everyone walked back to our sleeping bags, Howard shoved her in. She had all her clothes on. She hit her tooth on a log.

We got kicked out.

In high school Ute had so much pressure from his brother, Rain, to have sex. His brother made fun of him, and would get him drunk, and rip off his clothes, and tie him up. Ute finally had sex with Venus. The black guys made fun of Ute and Venus. They all wanted Venus.

*   *   *

The football players like Sam liked to make fun of Jews. He called people "Heebs" when they "Jewed" him. Sam played center on the team. He was fat and got no girls. He drank a lot of beer. Dave Frankel was Jewish and was on the team. He didn't say anything to Sam about all his talk.

In History our teacher, Mr. Tyson, did a reenactment of the Anne Frank story. It was an elaborate thing that he did every year. It was staged on top of the machine shop in the storage room. He made the storage room look like Anne Frank's attic. It was elaborate. Students played the Franks. At the end Mr. Tyson busted through the door dressed like an SS agent. He was pretty convincing.

When they kicked us out of camp, Hulk drove us to the Greyhound bus station in the middle of the night. Howard cursed at him the whole way. He called him a child molester and a little-dicked faggot. Hulk didn't say anything. Howard kept going for the whole ride; it took about an hour. Howard's face was red by the end. Whenever Hulk switched gears, Howard told him to "work that stick."

At the Greyhound station in Redding, Hulk bought us all tickets and put us on the bus. He watched as we drove off. I saw him walk away before the bus was out of sight.

Then we were in the dark bus with the real people, traveling in the middle of the night. Most of the people were Mexican, and were sleeping. We were all quiet; there was nothing left to do.

There was a layover in Sacramento. We got out and wandered around. There was a seedy hotel near the station called the Henderson Hotel. It made us think of a slut at our school called Alice Henderson and we laughed about it. They sold hot dogs and beer in the lobby. The guy behind the counter said that Axl Rose had stayed there once.

It was one in the morning.

When we went back to the depot, Ed and I had both lost our ticket receipts and we couldn't get on the bus. The woman in the customer service booth told us to go talk to the driver.

We went around to the side of the depot where the drivers had their lounge. Through the small window in the door we could see them. They were all black guys, sitting in there laughing and drinking coffee out of blue and white Styrofoam cups. They looked like they were having such a good time.

Chinatown
In Three Parts

Part I
Vietnam

It was Sunday, at the beginning of summer. I was at Jordan Middle School, playing soccer with the Mexicans on the field in back. They were all in their twenties and thirties; I was sixteen. They were gardeners and construction workers and cooks. It was sticky hot out.

After the game, I saw two girls smoking on one of the portable metal benches the coaches sit on. I walked over.

One was an Asian girl with a beat-up face and a nice-looking body. The other was pale white and tall with curly hair. The Asian one passed a cigarette to the pale one. They were my age.

I was sweaty.

"Hi, I'm Roberto." I put out my hand like a gentleman. The Asian girl smiled and said her name was Pam. We shook hands. The pale one smoked and didn't say anything, or even look at me. She was like a big drooping plant.

"How's the smoking?" I said.

"Fucking fine," said the drooping plant. She passed the cigarette to Pam and looked off, across the field. She blew the smoke out through a little hole in her lips.

" 'Fucking fine,' that sounds pretty good," I said. I smiled big. I said to Pam, "Can I try that fucking fine cigarette?"

Pam laughed without sound and handed me the cigarette. The other one looked over her shoulder like there was something very interesting over there.

"Mmmmm, that *is fucking* good," I said. "Fucking *fine.*" The drooping plant was not listening, only Pam was listening. She was pretty ugly, but when she smiled she wasn't so ugly. And I could see up close that she had a really good body.

"Hey," I said to the other girl. She didn't look back. "Hey, here's your cigarette." She still didn't look.

"Her name is Vicky," said Pam.

"Vicky," I said. "Vicky the hickey." She still didn't look. "Vicky, you remind me of a praying mantis," I said. "You're all long, and mantis."

Pam laughed for a second, and put her hand over her mouth like she shouldn't have. But then the mantis stood up.

"Pam, I'm going," said the mantis.

"Don't go," I said.

"Fuck you," she said to me. "Pam, are you coming?" she said. Pam didn't stand up.

"Pam doesn't want to go, mantis," I said.

"Screw you," she said to me. To Pam she said, "Pam?"

Pam said, "No," very quietly. The mantis turned and walked off across the field.

"Why don't you go pray, and eat some of your mates," I said to her back.

She walked crookedly and had a funny-shaped ass, like a heptagon.

I took another puff on the cigarette. It was a Camel. Some of the Mexicans called to me. They were carrying their soccer bags and water bottles at the other end of the field. They were waving. I waved.

I handed the cigarette back to Pam. She took a puff.

"Are you from around here?" I said.

She said she had just moved. She was going to start school with me at Paly in the fall. The pale girl worked at Midtown Video and they had met when she had gone in there to rent a video. She was the only person Pam had met so far.

I asked her which movie she rented.

Pretty Woman.

"I guess I ruined your one friendship," I said.

"She wasn't really a friend, just a girl."

"I know," I said. "Want to come to my buddy Tom's and smoke pot?" I said. She said sure. Tom lived close to Jordan.

At Tom's we smoked a lot of pot. Tom was there, we were in his room. We sat in a little circle near the open window and passed around a six-inch bong. We blew the smoke out the window. I got really high.

"Look at my eyes," I said. "I'm Chinese too."

She said she wasn't Chinese, that she was half Vietnamese and half Caucasian. Then she said, "I'm adopted."

I looked at her. I was so high.

"I love adoption," I said. She looked at me weirdly, then she laughed. I liked making her laugh, because then she wasn't so ugly.

"I love adoption *too*," said Tom.

We all laughed some more. Tom was tall and blond and handsome. The Sunday sun from the window was warm on my back.

We were sitting there, and then I said, as if it was the best idea I'd ever had, "Let's play 'Camping'!"

She asked what Camping was.

"Tom, go get a flashlight. And a sleeping bag. We'll pretend we're out in the woods, camping." Tom got up and went out to get the stuff. I went to the door and closed it, and turned off the lights. She was on the floor, watching me. I went to the window and closed the blinds, which made it pretty dark in the room. There was only the light from around the sides of the blinds, which glowed, a dull, radioactive orange. I took the comforter off the bed and went over to her.

"Roll up in this blanket with me, and we'll pretend it's a sleeping bag," I said. I laid the comforter on the floor. I opened my arms, and she got close to me. We lay on the comforter, I took her in my arms, and we rolled ourselves up in it. Our heads were covered too. We giggled.

Then I heard the door open. Tom was there, but I couldn't see him and he didn't say anything. He was standing there, and we were lying there. We were being quiet, as if he wouldn't know where we were if we didn't make a sound, as if we were out in the forest. We were giggling but we kept it in. Silent giggling.

"I got the flashlight," he said from the doorway. That really made us want to laugh, because it sounded like a question. Very quietly I said, "Shhh." Her face was right next to mine. She was holding on to me tightly.

Tom stood there, and then said, "Fuck you guys."

I heard the door close, and it was all dark again, except for the radiating window.

"We're camping," I whispered.

"Yes, we're camping," she said.

Then I whispered, "I heard that Chinese people have sideways vaginas."

She didn't say anything. Her face was touching mine, cheek to cheek.

"I'm Vietnamese, half," she said, like it was a secret, and like she hadn't told me before.

"Do you have a half-sideways vagina?" I whispered.

She said, "No," very quietly.

"Can I see?" I said. She was quiet, but not as long as before, and then she said okay. I took her pants off. We were still in our blanket, so it was hard to maneuver. I couldn't see in the dark, but I could feel. Her ass was fantastic, very hard. And her tits were big for an Asian. I spit on my hand, and then I put my dick inside her. It was good. And in the dark I couldn't see her face.

After—after I got her number, and after she left—Tom and I were in his room. We turned the lights on. It was dark outside now. He found a blood spot in the middle of the comforter.

I added it up. I had eighteen.

Part II
Headless

We talked on the phone a few times. She had just moved to Palo Alto. She was an orphan. She was half Vietnamese and half white, she had white adoptive parents. I didn't talk long on the phone, just enough to make her feel comfortable. She didn't talk much; I did all the talking. I was a nice guy. I'm a nice guy to everyone. I asked her questions. Her parents were both doctors. They lived in a big brown house near Castilleja, a few blocks down Embarcadero from the park with the wooden sculpture of the couple sitting on the bench. It was from France, and the couple was headless because Jason King sawed their heads off. He lived just across Embarcadero.

I called Pam one night and went over. She opened the door and came outside. Her parents were home. We went around the house to a shed in the backyard. She gave me a blow job in the shed. I asked her if she liked it. She said that she did. Then I left.

A week later, I was riding in Tom's car. Seth was there too. I said, "Let's go over to Pam's." Everyone said okay. I called her from a pay phone on University, then we went over. I knocked on the door. She came out.

"Hey, Pam," I said. We all walked down the street to the park. Tom Carver and Seth Klein are my best friends. I call Seth "Chunk," but he's not that fat, just short and chunky, and hairy. Rich and Jewish. He has a big dick.

Pam wore sweatpants and a T-shirt and a brown jacket that looked like a man's. We walked through the park, past the headless couple on the bench. A light was shining up from the ground at where the heads should have been, but they weren't there, they were hidden in Jason King's bedroom across the street.

We walked to the bowling green. The old people lawn-bowl there on Sundays. There's a place in the fence that is easy to slip through. I went through first, then Pam, then Seth and Tom. It was secluded in there. Just moonlight. On one side there was a big community house. It was white with green trim and the three stories of windows were dark. It was old. No one lived there.

Seth was excited, he was bobbling around. Tom was smiling big. He had big white teeth and a blond flattop. He had a Budweiser bottle that he had carried in his jacket pocket. His jacket was denim with a white fur collar. He was handsome.

Pam took off the brown man's jacket. She was in a white T-shirt, no bra.

Tom walked over to her. He was still holding his beer bottle. He just stood in front of her. She unbuckled his belt. Everyone laughed because we were excited. She unclasped his top button and unzipped his jeans. She took it out. She got on her knees in the middle of the soft, manicured bowling green.

After, Tom zipped up and walked back over to us, on the side. She stayed on her knees. Next, I walked over to her, before Seth, because I didn't want her to be too messy. She had to do it for a while. I made a mess. It got on her shirt and hair. I laughed, and Tom laughed. She was all messy for Seth.

Tom and I sat off to the side, on the ledge of the green. We shared the rest of his beer and watched.

Seth started talking to her.

"Baby, baby, baby, Klein is gonna explode on you." Everyone laughed. Even she laughed. "Ow," said Seth. We laughed even more, and she laughed even more, and he said "Ow" again, and we all kept laughing and it kept happening, until Seth had to push her off. She was laughing quietly. Tom and I laughed a ton, because Seth looked so mad. Chubby little devil in the moonlight. Finally she stopped laughing and finished. He did it on her face.

She was on her knees and wiped her face with her shirt. It was cold, and the big community house looked haunted. She stood up and we left the bowling green. The guys went to the car. I walked her to her house. She carried the jacket in her arms.

*　　*　　*

That summer, there wasn't much to do. It was just the guys a lot of the time. Usually we were over at Simon Kats's house. His mom worked nights as a nurse. Pam came over a couple times. She went into the bathroom and sat on the toilet. I went in and took her shirt off. Everyone lined up outside, and she blew everyone who went in there.

One afternoon we played football in the park next to the bowling green. Then we went to Jason King's house to get drinks. Jason's parents were gone. We were drinking sodas and vodka and smoking pot.

Pam came over. I got her into Jason's parents' bed. I got her naked. She wasn't even drinking. The guys lined up outside the bedroom. We went in, two and three at a time. Everyone fucked her. She got really messy. Some of the guys were so smelly. The room smelled like oysters. I kept going back in with everyone, like I was the party host. I didn't put my clothes on when I ushered people in. I was a wild monkey.

Toward the end, I got some vegetables from the refrigerator. I had carrots, and cucumbers, and a squash.

I squeezed past everyone who was standing at the door, watching. I took a raw wrinkly carrot and broke off the tip, so it wasn't too pointy. Jose was doing her doggy, and Angelo was in her mouth. Jose is half Mexican and Angelo is Filipino. I made Jose slow down; he was doing it real hard. I put the carrot in her butt. Everyone in the door was laughing like it was the best thing in the world. She let me keep it in there for a while. I moved it in and out. Then Jose and Angelo stopped, and we turned her over onto her back. I put a cucumber inside her. She didn't really want it, but I shoved it up there. I kept it up there for a while.

After, when she left, we burned the sheets in Jason's barbecue. There was a lot of smoke.

Part III
Caffe Buon

My dad's apartment building is near University Avenue. He owns the whole building. That's where I live. There is a restaurant down the street called Caffe Buon. It's Italian. I know the waiters, and the bartender, Al. Al said if I got him laid, I could have a free dinner.

I called Pam and I picked her up. I told her I was going to introduce her to someone. She knew what I meant. We went to Caffe Buon. It was five o'clock and Monday, so there were no customers.

Al was standing in the small circular bar in the corner. I introduced Pam to Al; they shook hands over the bar. Al was laughing, he asked her about school. The cooks peeked out of the kitchen to look at her. They're all Mexican. Al is Italian, and knows my dad. Al nodded to one of the waiters, Esteban. Then Al and Pam went to the back. Pam didn't look at me. She held Al's hand and they walked through a door next to the men's bathroom.

I sat at one of the tables. The place was empty. I had it all to myself. The waiter, Esteban, brought me a chicken dinner with farfalle. The chicken and the farfalle were under tinfoil. He brought a salad on the side. Farfalle is bow tie pasta, but it means "butterfly" in Italian. I ate and he brought me some red wine.

When I was almost done with dinner, Al walked out with Pam. She sat down at my table. The restaurant was still empty. I finished the rest of the chicken. Pam had a glass of water with ice. Al went into the kitchen and didn't come out. Customers started coming in for dinner and we left. I drove her home.

The rest of that summer, when I would walk over to University Avenue for coffee or cigarettes, I would see the Buon cooks and waiters outside smoking. They would always be sitting and leaning on this bus bench next to the restaurant. They told me to bring Pam by for them too. They said they would make me the best dinners if I did.

I did it one more time, for Juan the cook. He was short, and chubby, and had a baby's face and little baby hands.

I went over with Pam again. This time it was later in the evening than the first time, and there were customers inside eating, so we went around the side of the building to the kitchen door. It was a warm night.

As we walked up there was an orange glow spilling out of the side door where the kitchen was. Inside, through the screen door, I saw the two cooks were busy, but joking around too. It was Juan and a young one.

Esteban, the headwaiter, came into the kitchen to say something to Juan the cook. Esteban saw me and Pam looking in through the screen. He smiled and said something in Spanish. Then they all looked at us. The young cook said something to Juan in Spanish and they all laughed and made teasing noises. The young cook opened the door for us. I brought Pam in and introduced her to Juan. Juan didn't say much. He was looking at the ground. He had been in the middle of cooking something, but he went with Pam. They walked to the door next to the men's bathroom, where Al had taken her the other time.

I sat at a little table that was in the corner kitchen. It was where the cooks ate their dinners. The younger cook finished what Juan had been making and he made me some angel hair pasta with shrimp. It was good and had lots of garlic. I drank two glasses of wine with it. He was making me a steak cooked in butter when Juan came back with Pam. It hadn't been very long. Juan didn't say anything; he just walked back to his place at the stove. He took the steak that was cooking for me off the stove. Juan didn't look at me.

Pam was standing next to me. She didn't look at me, and she didn't say anything. Then the young cook came over and said that we should leave.

School started in September and Pam was there. She didn't have any friends. The only person she knew was me.

I tried out for soccer, and I made it on the team. At practice, I told the guys about Chinatown. That's what we started calling her. We'd all go down to Chinatown.

After I made the team, I had to go to soccer practice every day. It was boring. I stopped going and they kicked me off the team.

One day at lunch we parked Seth Klein's BMW in the far corner of the parking lot, behind the Palo Alto High School sign. I got Chinatown. I hadn't seen her in weeks. Ramone Washington came with us. He is a huge black football player. China got in the backseat. She was on her hands and knees on the seat. Seth got in behind her and put on a condom. He pushed her skirt up and took off her panties. Ramone stood at the open back door, in front of her face, and undid his pants. His dick is huge and disgusting. I was standing guard at the back of the car, looking at the school. Every once in a while I looked back. Seth was doing it really hard, and the car was shaking. Pam was choking. A bunch of cars left the parking lot at the beginning of lunch, and after a while they came back.

A month later, Seth's grandmother sent him away. He had been coming home drunk. His eyebrows would be shaved off, or he'd have felt marker beards and human shit on his face.

His grandfather had invented some sort of special part for microwaves. Seth's grandfather and parents are dead, but his grandmother is very rich. She sent him away to an expensive boarding school in Connecticut.

The night before Seth left, he spray painted TAKE ME DOWN

TO CHINATOWN on the wall outside the cafeteria, where they put all the rally posters. The next morning everyone at school saw it. Everyone started asking about Chinatown. Then everyone started hearing the stories. People thought I did the spray paint.

After that, Pam was different. She didn't talk to me anymore. She wore white dresses and did her hair differently. She made some friends: nerdy girls who worked on the school paper. People still called her Chinatown behind her back. And people like Jose and Angelo called her Chinatown to her face. "What's up, China?" they would say.

In March I got arrested. I hadn't talked to Pam in four months. Two police officers came into my typing class, fifth period. They told me to stand up; when I did they bent me over and pressed the side of my face down on the desk, next to my computer. They put handcuffs on me. One of the police officers was this Mexican lady cop. Her name was Maria Gonzalez.

They took me to the main office and questioned me in Dean Forest's office. Forest left so the cops could question me. They asked about all the times at the bowling green, and at Jason King's house, and at Simon Kats's, and about Caffe Buon, and the parking lot. And they asked about the vegetables. They told me they were arresting me for rape, and that they had arrested Seth in Connecticut. Maria Gonzalez said she was personally going to take me down.

But they couldn't do anything. Nobody had forced Pam to do anything. Later Seth and me laughed about it. They had called his grandmother and told her that her grandson was a sodomizer. His grandmother had to go to the hospital for a little while because of the shock.

They tried to shut down Caffe Buon. The cops accused them of running a prostitution ring in the back. But they couldn't do anything. They couldn't prove that Al had done anything with her. And Juan was gone by that time. He left the day after I took Pam over there.

After that, I left Pam alone. I'd see her in the halls, but she was someone different. It was like I didn't know her.

When we got older, I did things in my life and she did things in her life.

PALO ALTO II

April
In Three Parts

Part I
The Rainbow Goblins

I was driving Fred home from art class. It was a Wednesday night at about ten. Fred said, "That model was pretty hot tonight."

"She looked like a sick tree with a rotten knot."

"I'd fuck a tree," said Fred.

He never drew in art class. He came with me every Wednesday after school and sat there high until class ended. He didn't like to draw, so he just stared at the models. He even stared when they were naked men. One time, the teacher told him he had to draw, so he drew an explosion.

"So what would you do if you got into a car accident?" Fred said.

"Uh, I'd be pissed," I said.

"I know, but what if it was a drunk-driving accident, and you were the one who was drunk?"

"I'm on probation," I said. "I would go to juvie."

"I know, shitface, so what would you do? Fess up or drive away?"

"How bad is the accident?"

"It's bad, you crashed right into another car. But your car still runs." He was making gestures as he explained.

"Oh really?" I said.

"Yeah, the other person could be dead, or they could just be a little whiplashed, you don't know."

"Who is the other person?"

"You don't *know*, man! Look, you can either wait around and help the other person, and maybe it's Cindy Crawford and you fall in love, or you can get the fuck out of there. But you have to decide. Pretend like it just happened right *now*, what would you do?"

"Uh, I guess I would drive away," I said.

"*Really?* Drive away? That's your final answer?"

"Fuck it," I said.

"What a cowboy," said Fred.

* * *

That Friday after school, Fred and I went over to my friend Barry's house. It was still light out but we had a little party anyway. We all went in on a bottle of Kessler whiskey. April, this girl I liked, was at the party. I thought that if I got drunk enough, maybe some things would happen with her. I could tell her how I *really* felt and maybe by the end of the night I'd fuck her.

Barry and I and Fred and Ivan and A. J. Sims sat in the kitchen nook at the little table and took shots of the whiskey. It was strong and burned, and I felt powerful at that little table. When people would wander through the kitchen we'd get smart with them because the whiskey was working on us.

Chrissy came in to get a glass from the cupboard.

"Hey, Chrissy, you suck any dick lately?"

"You're a fucker, Ivan," said Chrissy. She was short, pretty, and perfectly blond. "Barry, why do you even let this fucker at your house?" she said.

"I dunno," said Barry.

"Chrissy, suck dick or get out," said Ivan.

"You're such a motherfucker," said Chrissy. "A *pale* motherfucker." Ivan was really pale.

"Suck *dick,*" said Ivan, and all the guys drinking whiskey laughed because Ivan had a running thing with Chrissy where he hated her and just said the worst things to her. Her boyfriend, Jerry, wasn't there so we felt free to laugh.

After a while I was drunk and things felt wavy. I felt like I could talk to April. I got up and wandered around the house. It was still daytime and there weren't that many people at the party. Some people were on couches drinking beer. I went through Barry's bedroom and out some sliding glass doors to the backyard. Ed was out there on the wooden bench on the deck. He was hunched over some tinfoil with the clear shell of a Bic pen. He was lighting the bottom of the foil and trying to suck up the smoke. There was no one else outside.

"What are you doing?" I said.

He sucked for a bit, then stopped, holding the smoke in. "Smack," he said.

I'd never seen anyone do heroin before.

"You seen April?" I said, and looked away. The yard was empty but I looked around anyway.

"There she is," said Ed. He was pointing back inside through the sliding glass doors. On the far side of the room, April and Barry were standing in the doorway to his bedroom, holding each other. Then their heads were slanted and they were kissing.

I walked to the front of the house. Fred was sitting on the brick step before the front door, smoking a cigarette.

"Let's get the fuck out of this place," I said.

He said okay and we walked down the driveway to my car.

"Where are we going?" said Fred.

"Fucking nowhere," I said, and drove faster.

I was at a stop sign at Middlefield, which was a pretty busy road, so I waited for a while. I was still angry. Then I drove forward and I saw the white car sink right into the front side of my car. It hit my car around the front tire, and there were some crashing sounds, and my car spun to the right, and then I was facing down Middlefield. For a moment I just stayed there. It was all very still, more than still. And then I was driving again, fast. In the rearview I saw the white station wagon with its front crumpled waiting in the center of Middlefield, diagonal to the road. Other cars were stopping. I turned off Middlefield onto a side street and my tires screeched and slipped, and when I pulled the car straight I raced down the block.

Fred said, "What the fuck is going on?"

"How the fuck did you know?" I yelled.

"What? Know what?"

"How did you know I'd get in a fucking accident?"

"I didn't! *What?* What are you talking about?"

"Fuck you, Fred! 'What *if?* What *if?*'"

Then he said quietly, "You're not really blaming me, are you?" I didn't say anything; the driving filled me. Then Fred said, calm and quiet, "Can I get out?"

I stopped really fast so that the wheels screeched and we slid. We were stopped in the middle of the street but no one was around. I didn't look at him. He opened the door and got out, and before he closed the door he said, "I'll see ya."

I drove, then I turned a corner and another corner, and I drove.

I drove past Nana's house. Then I was on El Camino and I drove past Stanford. I turned off El Camino and drove past my elementary school. While I drove I thought up ideas. I'd tell my dad that I crashed into a tree. I'd tell him I'd pay for the repairs.

Then the car started growling, the front right tire was rubbing against something. Then the hood was vibrating. I drove over to Colorado and then El Dorado and then a left on South Court and I was on my block.

Our house was at the end of a cul-de-sac. I didn't see my parents' cars.

When I pulled into my driveway, I saw a police car in Mrs. Bachman's driveway next door. While I was parking in my driveway, I saw the cop who went with the car. He was walking toward me. Like a gentleman, I got out of the car.

The cop was pretty small. He had an RFK haircut, and his eyes looked like they belonged to someone dumb.

"Hello," he said.

"Hi, Chip," I said. I don't think he heard me; he was looking at my car. The front was smashed and the white paint from the Volvo was mixed into the mangled gray metal.

"Whoo-eee," he said. "Seems like you're the one I'm looking for."

"Yeah, Chip," I said.

"Someone got your plates, buddy." Then into the radio he said, "I got 'im."

The backup came pretty quick. One and then two more and then there were five cars. A couple of the cops kept the lights flashing even after they parked and got out. Red was whipping everywhere, especially on the white of my garage door, round and round.

All the cops stood around me in their tight blue uniforms and the sky was golden above them. First RFK got my name and looked at my license. Then I had to hold my hand out and touch my nose while my neighbors watched. Another police cruiser slowed until it was in front of my driveway. There was a woman in the backseat with her face close to the glass. She didn't get out, but I saw her nodding. Her face was all jowls, thick and hanging. Then the car left.

"Walk along this line," said a tough lady cop pointing down at a line in the driveway. She had a square face and shorter hair than mine. Hers was combed.

I tried to walk along the line between the two slabs of cement in the driveway, but I couldn't. It was spinning and jumping.

"I can't," I said, and the words rolled around under my tongue.

I saw Mrs. Bachman hobble over to watch with the others. I was tired of being the show.

"Say the alphabet backward," said the tough lady cop.

"You say it," I said.

"If you're trying to get *wise* . . . ," she said, but she got interrupted.

"Looks like we got a *wise* one here," said the RFK cop.

"I'm not *wise*, Chip," I said. "I just can't say the ABCs backward, I can't even do it normally."

"Listen, smart-ass," said the tough lady cop, "you can do this sobriety test, or we can go down to the hospital and they can do a blood test on you. Your choice."

"I'm *drunk*," I said. "Take me downtown or wherever, I give in."

"Sir, I want you to say the alphabet backward. *Now*." Her arms were crossed over her chest, and underneath, her breasts filled out the tight blue shirt.

I looked around. There were a lot of neighbors now. All

the grown-ups and their kids, and Mrs. Bachman, her froggy, scowling face, with those red German cheeks, below that frumpy white hair.

Everyone waited solemnly; the lady cop looked as hard as Rushmore. I just wanted to go to Donkey Island where bad boys in leather jackets could smoke cigarettes and play pool and crash cars. I turned to the lady cop and said, "Z-Y-X . . . F-U-C-K U! U! U! U!" And I kept saying that letter while two cops bent me over the smashed-up hood of my Nissan Stanza. They cuffed me and walked me to the cruiser at the end of the driveway. The lady cop was shaking her head. The others guided me into the backseat, pushing down on my neck as I yelled, "U! U! U! . . . ," so loud. I tried to break Mrs. Bachman's hearing aid. If I could just reach those neighbors and tell them, "U! U! U!"

A month later, I went to court. My dad took me. I was assigned a lawyer. She told me I had to call the judge "ma'am" or "Your Honor." We waited for the judge and I kept hearing this line from this song in my head: *You down with O.P.P. (Yeah you know me)*. It had nothing to do with anything, but it kept going around in my head. Then the judge walked in from the side. She was in the black thing and had a thin face and glasses and long brown hair. She sat and looked at my police record and my school record.

"You know, Teddy," she said, "normally I get kids in here who can't multiply fifty by two, but you, you're smart."

"Thank you, Your Honor," I said. "O.P.P." was blasting.

She told me she ought to put me in juvenile hall, but it was hard to hear because of all those guys singing in my head. She said she would give me one more chance and make me a ward of the court, which meant I belonged to the state.

"If you do *anything,* if you are caught jaywalking, I will put you right into juvenile hall, is that clear?"

"Yes, sir," I said.

"Ma'am," said my lawyer.

"Ma'am."

"And as part of your probation, you'll do sixty hours of community service."

"Yes, ma'am."

"And you'll make an official apology to Miss Grossman, the woman you hit."

"Yes, ma'am." We got to leave and finally, on the drive home with my dad, those guys in my head shut up.

The next week I reported to my probation officer and set up a supervised apology with Sally Grossman. We met at the little place Sandwich Etc. in midtown, not far from where the accident had happened. Sally Grossman was fat, and she came with her fat friend, and there was a moderator there, Jake. He had combed white hair and a weak, kind face. We all had coffee and we sat around a small round table and looked at one another. I said I was really sorry. Sally Grossman looked like she liked that, but the fat friend looked angry.

Then Sally said, "Look, you have a problem. You're an alcoholic."

I nodded that, yes, I was.

"I can understand that," she said. "I have a problem too, eating. In some ways your problem is easier to deal with. I have to deal with temptation at least three times a day. You know?"

I said that, yeah, I did. Then Jake said that he had a problem too, that he had dealt with a gambling addiction. And that was it. The fat friend didn't say she had a problem. So we drank our coffee and Jake talked about the benefits of 12-step programs and I said that it sounded like a good idea and I would probably go soon. Then we were done and the next week I started my community service at the Children's Library.

The two old ladies who ran the library were nice to me. An old one with short brown hair in a bob was the assistant librarian, and a *really* old one with short gray hair in a curly flattop was the main librarian. The brown-haired one was named Judy; she was dry-skinned and thin. The other one was dry too, Mags; she didn't say much. They must have seen a little kid inside me, because they smiled at me like they smiled at all the kids who came in.

I walked to the library after school twice a week and on Saturdays. The old ladies would give me a cart of books to shelve. But after the first day, I just started reading all the picture books and didn't do the work. When the library closed at six, my cart of books would still be full, but the old ladies never said anything about it.

"See you soon, Teddy," they would say, and I'd tell them that they would. Sometimes when I was sitting on the floor reading, the old ladies would walk by the room. I know they saw me but they never mentioned it. There was a garden behind the library; they called it "The Secret Garden." There were sycamore trees in two rows and wooden benches with rounded cement frames. Sometimes I sat out there to think. But I didn't know what to think about.

I didn't talk to Fred for two weeks. I was a little angry that he had predicted the accident, but more because he had gotten out of the car, and even more because I was embarrassed about everything. One day, he showed up at the library. I was on the floor reading *The Very Hungry Caterpillar*. He sat down next to me and I read out loud to him. At the end the caterpillar turned into a butterfly. After that Fred came all the time.

One day, I started reading him *The Rainbow Goblins* by Ul de Rico. It was my favorite book when I was a kid. It's about this group of goblins that are each painted a different color of the rainbow and they hunt rainbows because they live off the juice of the rainbows' colors. The way they do it is they sneak up on the rainbows and they each lasso their designated color and then they drain the colors into their buckets and drink them. There are amazing pictures. Well, the goblins get sloppy and a field of flowers overhears their plans and then all the flowers of the valley conspire with the rainbow and the next day, when the goblins attack the rainbow, it disappears and the lassos spring back at the goblins and they're trapped in them and then the flowers secrete weird colorful juices, tons of them, and drown the goblins. One thing that was always interesting to me as a kid was that the goblins didn't wear underwear and when they drowned you could see the blue goblin's butt.

While I was reading this to Fred, sometimes my gaze

would catch a picture on the far wall. It was an image from *In the Night Kitchen*. Those three laughing bakers had such fat faces. Heavy-hanging cheeks and bulbous noses like genitals. I didn't want to look, but the picture kept grabbing my eye. Fred lay there with his eyes closed and his mouth open. He was higher than I was.

At the end of the book the rainbow vows to never touch the earth again.

"That shit was stupid. That was your favorite book?"

"Yes."

"Faggot," said Fred. He didn't open his eyes.

I looked up and saw those bakers again. They were cooking up the naked boy in a pie. I was happy there with Fred.

"Those fucking goblins were gay!" he said.

"Not so loud," I told him.

Fred didn't open his eyes. "They *suck* the juice out of rainbows? Rainbows stand for *faggots*."

"Shut up, Fred."

"What? They're *gay*! Rainbows are *gay*!" His eyes were a little open now.

"So?" I said.

"So, don't get all worked up over it. It's just a fact, you and the Rainbow Goblins are *gay*."

"Shut the fuck up, Fred," I said.

"What? They're a bunch of dudes, and they all hang out all the time. That's all they *did*, hang out together. All those dudes."

"So?" I said.

"And they lived together in a cave."

"So?"

"All in a cave! Gay! *Dirty* and gay," said Fred. As if he was the cleanest guy.

"Great fucking point, Fred. I mean, what children's book character *isn't* gay?"

Fred didn't answer. Then he said, "A lot of them."

"Cat in the Hat?" I said. "Gay. The Grinch? Gay. Hungry Caterpillar? He turns into a butterfly, gay!" Now Fred was thinking about it. I continued, "The Runaway Bunny, the bunny in *Goodnight Moon,* the Velveteen Rabbit, *Peter* Rabbit, all gay. All rabbits are gay."

"No."

"They're sensitive, but different, but also like boys, but then also not."

He thought, and then said, "Yeah, I guess they are."

"The little boy who flies around *naked* in *Night Kitchen,* and Max from *Where the Wild Things Are,* gay!"

"Bullshit, Max isn't gay."

"Bull true, he dresses up in his little white wolf suit, so gay. And then he tells his mom to fuck off . . ."

"That's not gay . . ."

". . . and then he goes to an island and hangs around with a bunch of monsters who party with him all night, dancing and parading him around on their backs."

"That's so weird, but I think it's kind of true," said Fred.

"All little-kids' stories have to be like that. They have to be all soft and gay, so that the moms are okay with it."

Fred sat there, and then he said, "*I* want a wolf suit."

"Yeah, me too," I said.

"I can't think of anything sexier than a skintight, furry

wolf suit," said Fred. He was really laughing a lot, almost too loud. Those three bakers looked like they were laughing too.

That night I had a dream. There were rainbows everywhere and I was driving all over town in my dad's busted car, wearing a white wolf suit. The car was making this horrible grinding sound with a whine underneath it. Whenever I hit another car, it just bounced off me and I would cackle.

Two days later, I went into the library to work. The place was empty as usual. I stopped at the front desk. Judy, the brown-haired one, was there.

"I really like it here," I said.

"We like *you,* Teddy," she said. "You're always welcome here, even after everything is over."

I said thank you and walked toward the back room. Down the hall, Mags, the gray-haired one, came out of the bathroom and slowly made her way toward me. When we passed, I smiled, and she smiled a wrinkled smile and said quietly, "Good boy, good boy."

Fred didn't come in. I rediscovered all the Bill Peet books. He usually wrote about animals and drew great pictures. I went through all of them. There was one about a hermit crab called Kermit the Hermit who hoarded all his stuff, and one about clumsy circus lions, and another about a little mountain goat with huge horns that he could ski on, and a peacock with a scary face patterned into his plume, and a pig with the map of the world on its side, and this clumsy beast that was part rhino, part giraffe, elephant, camel, zebra with reindeer horns called a Whingdingdilly. And there was this one about a dopey sea serpent named Cyrus that terrorized galleons.

It was good to read those books again; all the feelings came back to me.

> Once upon a time there was a giant sea serpent named Cyrus. Even though he was a horrible looking monster he wasn't the least bit fierce. All he ever did was wander about in the sea with no idea of where he was going.
>
> "I'm tired of wandering," said Cyrus one day. "I wish there was something more exciting to do. . . ."

Part II
Wasting

Things got bad at the Children's Library. I started taking the books home without checking them out and then not returning them. Sometimes Fred and I would get high and draw dicks and pussies on the animals in the books and then put them back on the shelves. One time I was in the Secret Garden and I tried to carve APRIL into the bench, but I didn't finish because one of the librarians came out, so the carving just said APRI, but the R was a little unfinished and the I was really light.

Then one day after school, my mom told me my probation officer wanted me to call her. I called from the kitchen phone while my mom washed vegetables in the sink. As the phone rang I watched my mother with the vegetables and I realized what a small woman she was.

"Hi, Janice," I said into the phone.

"Teddy, I'm gonna need you to come to my office on Tuesday after school."

"That's the day I go to the Children's Library."

"You're not going there anymore and you know it."

"What do you mean? I love that place," I said, and my mother looked over.

"Well, you screwed it up," she said. "I'll see you at three twenty on Tuesday. Don't be late, and you better not *drive* here."

My mother was holding half a green pepper. She looked so sad. The water ran in the sink.

On Tuesday, during first period auto class, Barry Chambers and Bill and I went out to the train tracks to try some of the weed that Barry had been growing in his backyard, on top of the shed. We walked down the tracks a little and stood near the Bat Cave. No Goth kids or anyone else was around. Barry had the stuff rolled in Saran Wrap. He unrolled it and there were two thick, glistening buds. Barry broke off enough for a bowl and filled his smooth porcelain rainbow pipe. The stuff was strong. When I coughed, Barry said, "See, I got the good shit." Bill took some and he coughed too.

"How'd you grow that?" said Bill.

"I just ordered the seeds from Amsterdam and followed instructions," Barry said. Barry was Mormon and cuddly like a sea lion and Bill was half Mexican and dumb.

After we smoked we sat on the rail of the tracks. The graffiti on the cement wall of the Bat Cave looked good. ORFN was up, and MSTK, and REVERS, written backward, and the best was LUST. With my eyes I kept tracing the way the letters flowed into each other. They were so well done I could taste them like chewy candy.

"What's up with you and April?" I asked Barry.

"April is crazy, but we're gonna fuck."

Bill had been quiet the whole time, but he said, "Yeah, *fuck* that shit." I guess he meant April was the shit and Barry should fuck her. His eye whites were pink and the veins were apparent. He was yukking.

I stood up and went to the wall. I had a black Sharpie in my pocket and I wrote SHIT FUCK COCK SUCK DIE ASS NOTHING-NESS MEANINGLESS CRY. My writing went a little over LUST, but he was big and in red spray paint.

"What does all that mean?" said Barry.

"Nothing," I said, but it was something. Barry let us use his Visine and then we went back and made it before the end of auto class. I banged on the side of an engine with a hammer and then I sat in a metal chair. In English, I looked at a book but the words didn't separate; all the letters were ants marching into the crease.

After school, the weed was wearing off and I walked with Fred toward the court building where Janice had her office. It was near California Avenue, so we just walked down El Camino. Fred had been doing crazy things lately. Stupid things, like throwing rocks through house windows at night, and then running.

"Can you believe that Barry is gonna fuck April?" I said.

"No," Fred said. Fred had never fucked, and I had only once. It was with Shauna. Everyone called her Dog Bite Shauna because a dog had bitten her and there were two horizontal scar lines on the left side of her face. We did it at a party, and when I was finally on top of her I closed my eyes because her face was so close. We kissed while we did it and I remember being surprised because I was holding her face and I couldn't feel the scars, but when I opened my eyes they were there.

"*Barry?* I mean why Barry?"

"I don't know, cuz he's a fucker," said Fred. "And he's nice."

"But *Barry?* He's, like, chubby and he's *Mormon* and . . . I mean, I don't think he's ever fucked before. Why does she like him?" We thought while we walked.

"He plays drums," said Fred.

"Whatever," I said, and we walked in silence. On a public mailbox I drew a face with my Sharpie. It was a mournful face, and next to it I wrote,

> FUCK INTO THIS
> BORN INTO THIS

At California Avenue, Fred went into the café at the Printer's Ink bookstore to get coffee and I walked on to the court building. It was three thirty already.

I went to the seventh floor and checked in and then waited in a wooden chair for Janice. I wasn't high anymore but I was so tired I kept my backpack on when I sat. I was slumped to the side of the chair when she came out.

"Okay, Teddy." I stood up. "Nice shirt," she said. I had a red plaid shirt on and the pocket was ripped so it hung funny. She was fat, and wearing tan pants. When she turned, her ass was this huge ugly thing that was wide and flattened from sitting. In her office, I took my bag off and sat in the heavy wooden chair across the desk from her.

"So," she said, and then was very still. Her face was like her ass, flat and wide. Her cheeks stuck out farther than her temples and they hung like the jowls of a Saint Bernard. Her skin was oily and olive-colored with splotches of red around her nose.

I didn't say anything. The walls were beige and the ceiling had those white squares with little holes in them. It was the most boring place I had ever been. Finally she asked me if I was high and I said I wasn't and she said she could test me if she wanted to and I told her that would be okay, but she didn't say anything more about it. Then she said, "You drew a dick on the Runaway Bunny?"

"No, that was Fred," I said.

She asked who Fred was but I didn't answer. "Did you have friends visit you while you were doing community service at the Children's Library?"

"No, no one came, it was *me*. I'm sorry I drew the dick on the Runaway Bunny, and the vagina on the mom bunny. It was really stupid, I'll pay for the book."

"Yes, you will, of course you will, but you're not doing the rest of your hours there. The librarians don't want you there anymore."

"They like me."

"No, they don't. You're lazy and you carved 'ape' into their bench outside."

I started laughing. It seemed really funny at the time so I kept laughing. Maybe I was still high. "I didn't write 'ape,' I wrote 'apri.'"

"What the hell is 'apri'?"

"Nothing, just some shit."

"Well, you're paying for that too," Janice said. I said okay, and she asked what kind of asshole I was, defacing libraries. I said I didn't know. Then she handed me a list of places where I could finish my community service hours. I had thirty-two hours left. I could work at Goodwill, I could clean up graffiti, I could work at Planned Parenthood.

"Goodwill sounds okay," I said. She was looking at her own copy of the list.

"No, actually you don't get to choose," she said. "You're working at Sycamore Towers." Sycamore Towers was a nursing home. My great-grandfather had been there before he died at Stanford Hospital. I used to visit when I was about three and he'd always give me chalky candies. "Great-grandpa candies," we called them. There is a photograph of him and me shaking hands in the doorway to his room: he is tall, in a gray suit, with white hair; and I'm in a diaper, standing on my toes to reach his hand.

I started working at Sycamore Towers. It had fourteen floors; I worked on the twelfth. There was a desk station for the orderlies in the center of the floor, and from there the four wings extended out in each direction, so the place was shaped like a crooked cross. Each wing held eleven rooms for the residents: five on one side of the hall and six on the other. Near the orderlies' station there was a community room where the old people worked on crafts, and across the hall there was a TV room.

Most of the old people were in wheelchairs and they didn't move much. They usually sat dispersed about the four halls doing nothing. There were also some that lay in bed all day and had bedpans. Except for the meals and craft time, the old people were left to themselves. Some watched TV in the TV room and a few read, but most stared at nothing.

On Tuesdays and Thursdays I'd walk to the Towers after school. I'd get there around three thirty because it wasn't very far, over near University Avenue. When I arrived at the Towers the old people would be having their craft time in the community room. I would sit with them and make sure they had their beads and crayons, and if anyone needed water I would get it. They would do crafts for an hour and then they were free until dinner at six. I would push them around in their chairs and clean up after them and get supplies from the storage room for the orderlies.

There was another kid working off community service hours; his name was Brian and he went to the other high school, Gunn. He was Asian, and had a tall head and a square haircut, so he looked like a number 2 pencil eraser. He was a smart kid but he had two hundred hours of community service because he made a bomb at school.

One afternoon when he and I were in the elevator bringing up packs of toilet paper from the basement, I asked him about the bomb.

"It wasn't a bomb," he said, like he had been waiting for me to ask. "It was supposed to be a joke. I mean, I'm good at chemistry and I knew what I was doing, I've done it a bunch of times before. It was supposed to be a smoke trick, that's it. All this smoke was going to come out of the drinking fountain, and everyone would get scared, big deal. But the guy I did it with fucked up and put the pipe too far into the fountain, so there was no room for the smoke to get out and the whole thing exploded."

"Oh fuck," I said.

"It was bad. The cement went flying and there were flames and a bunch of backpacks got completely melted and a few kids got burned on their backs and heads. One girl had her hair burned off on one side."

"That's horrible," I said.

"Yeah. What's worse is I got expelled. And I was supposed to go to Duke next year, and they pulled my scholarship."

For a smart guy Brian seemed dumb, the way his huge head bobbed around when he talked. Just before we got to our floor he asked me if I liked the old people.

"They're okay," I said. "They're just like big children."

"They fucking smell," he said, and then the bell dinged and the doors opened and he walked out.

Crafts for the old people usually meant drawing with crayons, or stringing beads, or making cat's eyes with yarn. At first I just sat and watched; their weak fingers had difficulty gripping things and some of their wet mouths hung open. On the third week I started drawing them. I had put in a lot of time in drawing classes, especially since the last arrest. In the evenings I didn't work with the old people, I would go to life drawing and portraiture classes at the Palo Alto Art League. It was just this cool old building that was actually pretty close to the Towers. My teacher, Mr. Wilson, was this wily old guy with a beard like a wizard who wore all denim, every day.

I started bringing my sketchbook and sketching pencils. I usually just drew the old people's faces. I would draw life in their eyes even though many of their lights had gone out. I would capture their decaying skin with as much realism as possible. Wrinkles within wrinkles, blotches, hair in wisps. And their necks like fowls': bone protrusion, saggy-soft flesh, goiters. I drew all of the people on my floor many times. The orderlies didn't care that I hardly helped because they were worse than I was. They were all young, and argued in Spanish and laughed around the orderly station; and the guy orderlies would tease the girl orderlies, and they all would flirt; but when they dealt with the old people they were mean and cold, as if all the old people were animals.

"Those are cool pictures," Brian said. "They make me think of death."

"I'm trying to draw them with some dignity. It doesn't seem like anyone else cares," I said.

"It's hard, man. Who wants to care for someone who has lost his mind and motor skills and can't take a shit without help? That's why you have all these stupid assholes here, to wipe their asses for them."

"But the orderlies don't care about these people."

"No shit, *because* they have to wipe their asses and change their bedpans and listen to their insanity *every* day; we only have to be here twice a week. Imagine if you were here every day."

"I hope I die before I ever come to a place like this," I said. Brian said I probably would because I smoked cigarettes.

I drew one woman more than all the others. Her name was Tanya. I liked her because of her smile and her eyes. That was all, she wasn't any smarter or more coherent than the rest of the old people. She just radiated kindness.

I'd draw her in all different ways. Her face with its cross crinkles, like bunched cloth around her eyes; her mouth: wrinkly soft from so much smiling. I'd draw her full-bodied; grinning in her wheelchair, sitting over the beads that she would thread and drop, which bounced, sharp-sounding, on the floor; or in the TV room, hunched in her sweater: bird-like, brittle, her chair angled slightly away from the television because she wasn't really watching. And her smile always like a child's.

One Thursday, during craft time, when they were all coloring with their crayons, I placed two of the drawings I had made of Tanya on the table in front of her. Tanya was working on a red house; the jagged red scribbles shot all over the page and into the blue mountain she had drawn in the background. When I put the pictures down she stopped with the crayon. The color was called "Watermelon." She looked at my pictures. They were good; one was of her face and caught her warmth, the other was a picture of her in her chair, hunched and staring at nothing. She picked one up and then the other, and then she cooed.

"Ooooh, these are nice, very nice. I don't play with games, but I like this so much. My daughter come, and she walk good." Then Tanya put them down and was drawing again. I thought she had already forgotten about me, but as she was going over the jagged marks of the barn with Watermelon, she said, "I'm drawing a barn. The place I grew up in when I was a little girl. My daddy said, when peacetime come to the horses, then we all sleep. Sleep, sleep good, you think?" And then she stopped drawing and looked at me like she wanted an answer.

"Sure," I said, "sure," and she smiled and all the warmth I liked came into her face, and then she went back to drawing.

The next day was Friday. In auto class Barry said his parents were leaving for some Mormon thing and he was thinking about a get-together at his house that night, not a party but a group of people to celebrate the full harvest of his plant. I said I would think about it, but I knew it would be him and April all over each other.

After school I went to the Art League like I usually did on my days away from the Towers. I had a class from four to seven and another from seven to ten. It was me and a bunch of older people and one young Asian girl who was pretty good. There was one model per class. In the early class the model was a guy named Ogden who was about fifty-five; his body was muscular but his skin hung a little loose. The teacher, Mr. Wilson, walked around with his gray beard and bald head, and denim shirt tucked into his jeans. He would lean over and give suggestions to people.

I was drawing in a different way than I usually did. Usually I would try to be as exact as possible, like a Renaissance painter, but all that seemed like bullshit suddenly. The drawings of Tanya did something to me. I think I had really captured her, they were my best drawings, but it didn't mean anything. Everything was changing, things felt different, but I wasn't sure why. I was drawing Ogden in a much looser way than I usually did. Usually I would just do one drawing per pose, but I was doing five to ten and letting them drop on the floor. Mr. Wilson stood next to me and held his chin in his hand.

"Going fast. Really fast," he said. I said I was and kept drawing.

"You know, Picasso drew fast," he said. "He could draw a dove in sixteen seconds, and they're great, right?"

"The doves? Yes."

"But that sixteen seconds had six *decades* of work behind it," he said, then he dropped his hand from his chin and smiled through his beard. Most of the other students had heard him because he talked pretty loudly, and they all approved of his wise observation, grunting and saying, "Ahhh," and "Oh, how true, how true it is." Wilson went on: "Picasso started off painting in a classical style, but it was only after he had *mastered* the *masters* that he broke tradition and became Picasso. He knew he had all the skill of Raphael at age sixteen, but that wasn't enough. Technical skill is never enough. He needed to find his *voice*. We all have a voice or a style, but it takes practice, practice to find it. The technical stuff needs to become second nature." Everyone agreed with this part too. Wilson said quietly to me, "You remind me of Sylvester Stallone." I stopped drawing. Wilson went on: "I used to go to art classes with him. He was always trying to break away from classical form."

One of the ladies spoke up. "Sylvester Stallone, the *actor*?"

"That's right. He's a huge art enthusiast and not a bad artist either." Everyone was surprised and talked about it for a bit. Someone said that underneath all that muscle he was actually a really intelligent guy. "He did write *Rocky,* after all."

During the Stallone discussion, Ogden held his pose. I tried not to listen and draw, but something had gone out of me. I picked up a few of the drawings that had dropped to the floor. They looked like a kid's drawings, except they were of a naked man.

In the second class we had a woman, Beth. She was about forty and large: her breasts hung heavy and low so that the skin stretched thin at the top of them, and her belly had folds. She was great for drawing, but I wasn't in the mood. Wilson had killed my motivation for the fast drawings, but I didn't have the patience to do it the old meticulous way either. I wanted to leave but I didn't know where I wanted to go. I just drew her belly and shaded it and went over it again and again until it wasn't any good. I thought about bodies decaying and my own life shriveling.

Wilson was going on about his near-death experience again. He had had open-heart surgery six months before and almost died. He loved to talk about it, and the ladies and old guys loved to hear it.

"... It's true. I don't care how much attention we devote to the *body* in here, I *know* there is a spirit, I *experienced* it. Whatever it is that makes me *me* had lifted away from this earth-bound state and I was on my way, I was *on my way*." He was laughing at his own enthusiasm and some of the women were laughing too; a few had stopped drawing to listen. "Excuse me, Beth, for talking about the body so much while you're posing for us, but I think we should all think about this *while* we draw the body. The body is the vehicle for the *spirit*. We can't draw the spirit, we can only draw physical things, but *through* those physical things you might be able to intimate something of the spirit *underneath*. At least *try*, don't just draw Beth, draw her *soul*. Because it's *there*. I am telling you, when I was going toward that light, something said, 'Cy, nope. Nope, nope, nope, you're getting a first-class tickeroo back to earth, you better do good by it.'"

Usually I liked Wilson, but he seemed different now, like a clown. After class, I stuffed all my drawings into a trash can. Beth came out of the bathroom with clothes on and saw me trashing the drawings of her. She was wearing blue sweatpants and a black hooded sweatshirt like she was a regular person. She didn't say anything.

Instead of going home, I started walking toward Barry's house. I didn't care if April was there, I was ready to get high and not think about anything. The night was cold and I hunched with my hands in my pockets and my sketchbook under my arm, and there was a low orange moon, almost full, and huge because it was so low. And I didn't care.

I got to Barry's a little after ten thirty; I walked through the ivy-lined pathway on the side of the house, and the heart-shaped leaves against my face were cold. At the back of the house the curtain was closed behind the sliding glass door that led to Barry's room. I heard voices and I tapped lightly. Barry's sea lion face appeared, scruffy and round. When he saw it was me he smiled and slid open the door.

"Welcome, motherfucker," he said. It was warm and dark inside. He had his lights off and his blacklight on, so the Zeppelin poster and the Crumb KEEP ON TRUCKIN' . . . poster were glowing in bright greens and pinks. On the floor there were about eight people sitting in a circle.

"Teddy," someone said, "siddown and get ready for the magic carpet ride." I sat down and I saw that it was Bill. He put his arm around me for a second and squeezed my shoulder. He must have been excited because that was a lot of talking and touching for him. Fred was also there, and Ed, and Ivan, and Ute, and Jack Canter, and Tim Astor. No girls; no April. Barry continued packing his green three-foot bong.

"The skull bong!" said Fred. And everyone else said, "The *skull bong*!" Because the bowl of the bong was shaped like a grinning skull.

"And the official first crop of the Chambers homegrown!" said Barry, and everyone cheered. Then he put the bong to his mouth and lit the bowl, and in the light from the flame his round face turned orange as he sucked and the water bubbled, and the glass of the base was thick with smoke. Barry pulled on the stem and the smoke went up into his throat. He held it in and made little guppy sounds and then let it out and coughed and everyone cheered.

The bong went around, and when it got to me I sucked as hard as I could, and when I saw the green tube was packed tight with smoke I sucked it up like a soul. It went right to the center of me and I knew that that one hit was going to take me over. I let it out and choked hard and by the time I got my breath back I was already high. I didn't mind Bill or Fred or anything. The bong kept going around and I started smiling.

Bill patted me on the back again. "See, Teddy, all is *gooood*. It's like we're at the fucking *beach*."

"The beach?" I said. Bill was smiling so big, so many teeth.

"Yeah," he said, and giggled. "Can't you feel the sun, buddy? We're at the fucking beach." He really liked that idea because he was looking up at the ceiling with his arms spread as if there was a sun up there and he was soaking up the rays.

"You're a Mongoloid," I told him. He laughed.

"A mongo-what?" he said, but he didn't want an answer because he started laughing and couldn't stop.

Then across the circle Fred said, "Hey, Barry, where the fuck is April? Did you fuck her yet?"

Everyone got interested and Barry was quiet for a second. Then in a low voice he said, "Yeah, I did."

"No shit? Did the deed?" said Jack. "Your fucking first, right?"

"Yeah," said Barry, but he was being a little shy.

"That's fucking great," said Bill. "I told you to fuck that shit!" and he started laughing at himself again. Everyone congratulated Barry: "Nice one," "Good work, pimp," "She's fucking hot," "That *ass* . . ." He let them say their stuff for a minute, and then he said, "No, it's bullshit."

"You *didn't* fuck her?" I said.

"No, I did, but the whole situation is bullshit. She's fucking crazy. I mean *really* crazy. Like I think she got molested or something."

"Why the fuck would you say that?" I said. "Did she tell you?"

"No, but I can just tell," he said.

"Wadda you mean?" I said. "You mean you're just making that up because you *think* you can tell."

"You *can* tell those things," said Fred.

"Oh, shut the fuck up, Fred, no you can't," I said. "And how the fuck would you know, you little troll, you haven't been with a girl in your life."

"Fuck you, Teddy," said Fred. "You've only been with Horse Face, Dog Bite Shauna Woo." Everyone laughed and oohed.

"Shut up, Fred," I said. "You don't know shit." And that was the end of it. I couldn't bring up April again. Barry had done it with her, the girl I loved, and it had meant nothing to him; Tanya would die and no one would care; and there were billions of bodies alive on earth and they would all be buried and ground into dirt; and Picasso was a master at age sixteen and I was a perfect shit.

Everyone smoked more and we listened to music. Bob Marley was on and there was a line in a song he kept repeating: "The stone that the builder refuse / Will always be the head cornerstone." After the third time he sang it Barry asked everybody what they thought it meant.

"It's from the Bible," I said. "The meek will inherit the earth, or something like that."

"Why will the meek inherit the earth?" said Ute. "I never understood that."

"Jesus said it," said Jack.

"I know, but *why?*" said Ute. "Why will they? And how?"

Ed said, "They *won't*."

Everyone thought about that and shut up.

I had a bad weekend. I didn't do anything. I just watched *Point Break* again and read some of *Crime and Punishment*. On Tuesday I went back to the Towers after school. I was almost done with all my hours, and then I knew I would never go back there. When I got to twelve Brian was there, carrying the television. The screen was cracked and there were dark spots behind the cracks. The TV wasn't big but Brian was struggling a little.

"Hey, help me with this thing," he said. I took one end and we carried it together into the elevator. "One of the zombies fell on it and knocked it over."

"Is everyone okay?"

"Yeah, I think so. The guy was fine. They won't even miss it; they can't understand what they're watching anyway."

"Yes they can."

"Are you kidding me? Those people are *gone*. They don't know what's happening. Two of them thought I was their son, and I'm *Chinese*."

"They're still people."

"Whatever that means. The more time I spend here, I think more and more about how they're just these bags of guts being wheeled around, and it's like the gears are turning inside, but just out of habit, nothing is alive."

At the ground floor we went outside and around to the

back where the Dumpsters were. We did three windup heaves and then let the TV go into the back of one of the Dumpsters. The screen shattered and the body settled among the papers and cardboard.

Back upstairs, one of the orderlies came up to me. His name was Manuel, he was about twenty-five, and had a kind face.

"Hey, Tanya's daughter came by and saw the pictures you made of Tanya. She liked them."

"Really?"

"Yeah, you should go see her. Room twelve twenty-six."

I walked over to Tanya's room. Inside, it was dark. The overhead light was on, but it was weak and had a green cast. There were two beds in the room; Tanya was sitting on the edge of one, staring at the floor. The other bed had a naked mattress on it. I said hello and she looked up, and when she saw it was me she gave me her smile. I walked over and sat on the empty mattress across from her. Our knees were almost touching because the room was so small.

Then I noticed the two pictures framed on the wall behind her. They looked like a memorial.

"How are you?"

"Fine. I fine," she said, smiling.

"I see you put the pictures up," I said.

"Pretty. You draw so well."

"No. I think I'm crap," I said. "Sorry, I mean, I'm no good."

She slowly reached over and took my hand. Her hand felt like sticks in a sheet. She cradled my hand with both her hands.

"You good," she said. "You so good, a good boy." She lifted my hand and held it to her face. Her cheek was softer than I expected. I moved my thumb around a little and felt her wrinkles. They were just there, skin folding on itself.

"You good," she said again. "You captured me good."

She smiled and I felt the soft skin bunch under my fingers. I looked into her smile. There was someone in there.

Part III
April

Right before eighth grade I moved from Phoenix to Palo Alto with my parents and older sister, Tiff. My dad came to work at ROLM. I could play soccer and I smoked more than anyone. But in Palo Alto, even when the other soccer girls were nice to me, something didn't fit.

Mr. B was my soccer coach. His first name was Terry, and his last name was Brodsky. He'd been "Mr. B" for years, he said. He was forty-two. He had all his hair and tan skin and wore a purple baseball cap a lot. After a week, he told me I was the best soccer player in the eighth grade. He told jokes about dogs and horses and skeletons and I laughed at them. "A skeleton walks into a bar and says, 'Give me a beer and a *mop*.'" The ones about horses were even worse, and sexual, but I laughed. He would also make fun of the boys in my class. "I saw Teddy Morrison changing the other day and I think he's missing the hair under his arms, " then he'd laugh.

After two months in Palo Alto I had made some friends, Shauna, Sandy, and Alice Wolfe. And our soccer team was doing well. At the end of practice one day, Mr. B asked me to babysit his son, Michael. "I have a date this Saturday," he said. "I know, *stupid*." I told him it wasn't stupid.

"I don't know why I even try, it's going to be dumb."

"I can't Saturday, Shauna is having her bat mitzvah."

"*Bat mitzvah?* Ha." He was sweating at his temples from coaching us. "You going to go make out with some Jewish dudes at the bat mitzvah?"

"No, but she's my friend."

"I know she's your friend, she's great—a little horsy in the face, but—no, sorry, that's mean, I didn't mean that. Look, you should go, but if you did this for me, I'd consider it a personal favor. I don't think I'll be out late. I'm going out with a *teacher*. Just bring your dress and you can change at my place and I'll drive you to the party after."

I thought about it and then I said okay. Shauna Woo was on the team. She was nice, but also just a girl. Her dad was Asian and her mom was Jewish. She was rich and she had just about everything, but she had been bitten on the face by a dog when she was younger. There were two jagged lines across her left temple and the top of her cheek.

On Saturday I went to Mr. B's at five thirty and he left for his date. His son, Michael, was five, he had a round head that was a little pointy on top, and unlike Mr. B he was blond. He was nice but he was just a kid, empty and selfish. He sat on the floor and looked up at the TV and played his video game.

"What are you playing?"

"The Legend of Zelda." He was controlling a green elf walking around a graveyard.

"What are you doing with that flute?"

"It's an ocarina. It does stuff. Like, you can call fairies, or call your horse." The elf played a song on the flute and day turned to night and then lightning hit a grave and it exploded. Then the elf jumped into the grave.

My older sister, Tiff, had given me a joint for the weekend and I went out on the porch and lit it. It was nice to smoke alone. I leaned on the wooden rail and it was wet from dew but I leaned on it anyway. The sky was black with a dark blueness at the horizon, and different from a Phoenix sky, sadder. I watched the blueness sink below the houses until there was only black and stars. I smoked half the joint and licked my fingers and put out the end and put the unsmoked half in my Reds pack. I lit a cigarette and sucked hard. Shauna and everyone were at the party already. She had become a woman that day, but she would always have her scars.

When I went back in Michael was still playing. The elf was riding on a horse, galloping across a grass valley. I told Michael he should stop playing so we could watch a movie. Mr. B had a videotape of *Fast Times at Ridgemont High*. Michael said he wasn't allowed to watch it but I let him. We sat on the couch together. Sex in a baseball dugout, sex in a pool house, an abortion. The joint made all of it funny. Michael didn't laugh or say anything. He was really quiet when the boobs and vaginas came out. Then it ended.

"I don't want to go to bed," he said. I picked him up and

carried him into his room. I put him under the blankets and I lay next to him above the blankets. I guess he should have brushed his teeth but I thought, "Fuck it." There was nothing to say because he was a little kid. I stared at the ceiling. I thought about my sister. Sometimes we laughed so much that I thought we'd never stop. But we hadn't done it much lately; she had a boyfriend now. Then Michael was asleep.

At eight Mr. B came home. "What are you watching?" he said. I was watching *Cheers*. He sat on the couch a little away from me. On TV Cliff was joking with Norm and Sam. He said, "Well, ya see, Norm, it's like this. . . . A herd of buffalo can only move as fast as the slowest buffalo. And when the herd is hunted, it is the slowest and weakest ones at the back that are killed first. . . ." He was going to tell a joke but Mr. B started talking. "Well, that was a shitty date."

"What happened?" I said.

"*Nothing*. That's the thing with teachers, it's always *nothing*. Boring. I feel like I'm back in school or something. I can't believe you have to listen to those people every day. At least I can go home if I want." He laughed at his joke.

"I *don't* listen," I said.

"You don't? You listen to *me*."

"Well, yeah, of course I do *that*, Coach." I smiled because I liked him.

"You fucking *better*," he said. We both laughed and he told me to get dressed and he'd drive me to the bat mitzvah.

"What about Michael?"

"He'll be fine, it'll take five minutes. It's over near Gunn, right?"

I went into the bathroom and put on the dress. It was light lavender. It was my sister's and too big for me in the boobs.

I walked out and Mr. B stood from the couch.

"You look amazing," he said, and walked over. I said I hated dresses, but he wasn't listening. When he was near me he put his thick hands on the bottom of my face and tilted his head to the side; he kissed me. His face was close, and I smelled a strong smell, and everything seemed full, and bigger, and his chin was scratchy, and his lips were full of a thickness of feeling; he held his lips on mine for a long time. Then he pulled back, looked into my eyes.

"You shouldn't smoke so much," he said. And then he kissed me again. An older person, but still a kiss. His mouth opened and I knew that part; his tongue came through like a little fish and I met it with my tongue. Everything was thick inside my mouth.

"April, you're the most important person to me."

"*Me?* Why?"

"When you get to be my age, there is nothing you appreciate as much as a real person. You're *real.*" We kissed one more time, softer, and then I said we should go. We went out toward his purple-blue 4Runner. When I went around the side of the car, I lost sight of him for a moment, and the streetlamps flared in their plastic coverings.

He drove me over to the temple. We listened to Jimi Hendrix and didn't say anything. Jimi was along the watchtower and the streets were glistening with wet. At the temple Mr. B pulled into the lot and there was a large unexpected bump because the entrance was slanted in a strange way, and we both jerked forward. He turned the car and parked us in a corner where it was dark.

"I really fucking like you, April."

"I like you too," I said. We sat there and there was moisture in his eyes, glistening from the dashboard lights.

"When you know life like I do," he said, "you know that there isn't much that is good. But I know that you're good. Really good." One of the lights in his eyes was red. I said thanks and he kissed me on the cheek and told me I should go. I got out and started walking across the parking lot. Mr. B's car turned and drove out over the dip and into the road; red taillights into black.

The lot was dark but there was a pulsing glow coming out of the high windows of a building across the lot. Then I could hear music. I took out my pack of Reds and slipped one into my mouth and lit it with my little black lighter. The cigarette was good after kissing Mr. B. I walked toward the building with the glow. I wasn't good. I was regular, or worse.

Someone called to me. I saw it was Teddy off a ways in the darkness. There was also a person crouched on the ground near him. That was Ivan. Ivan's face was so pale. I asked what they were doing. I got closer. Ivan was holding a bullet on the ground and was tapping the back of it with a thin hammer. I stood a little away.

"Should you really be doing that?" I said.

"Shut the fuck up, they're my stepdad's," said Ivan.

"I don't care whose they are," I said. "Isn't it bad to have bullets at a synagogue?"

Teddy laughed. "Well, it's not even fucking working." He

was wearing a black dress shirt and had gel in his hair. He looked nice. He always did. Ivan was always pale and scary. "Why are you so late?" Teddy said.

"I was babysitting," I said. Ivan kept tapping.

"Oh, well, the party kind of sucks, old people and bad dancing. Want to go across the street to Gunn and drink?" Gunn was the other high school, the one we wouldn't go to the following year.

"Let me see Shauna first," I said. I went over to the building with the music and the lights and stood in the doorway. Inside, people were dancing to ABBA's "Dancing Queen," fast and awkward. Some people were laughing. There was a long table along the side of one wall with lots of food and cakes. I had never been to a bat mitzvah. In Phoenix I didn't know any Jews. I saw Shauna across the room of bodies. She was dancing and laughing with her mom and brother. She had a bunch of makeup on. So much I could hardly see the two scar lines.

I saw other girls from the team but I didn't want to talk to any of them. They all knew Mr. B.

I walked back into the dark and told Teddy I wanted to go to Gunn.

Ivan picked up his bullets and put them in his pocket. We walked down a hill in the dark and I could hear the bullets clinking in Ivan's pants.

When we passed the cemetery, Ivan said, "That suicide guy just got buried there."

"How do you know?" I said.

"He *did*, or what's left of him," said Teddy. The kid had stepped in front of a train at the East Meadow crossing.

"My stepdad knew his dad," said Ivan. "Said he was a prick, probably why the kid killed himself."

We walked across Arastadero to Gunn. There was a large electronic billboard on a post. Above the electronic part there was a black part with fancy red lettering that said GUNN and TITANS. The electronic part said, BEAT PALY! GO TITAN FOOTBALL. 10/10, 6 P.M. Paly was going to be our high school the next year.

We walked through campus. The buildings were made of cement, and in the dark the place was like a bunker. We made our way through the shadows to a grassy area. In the center was a huge oak tree that rose above the roofs of the classrooms. There was moonlight all around and it made the top of the tree silver-white. The ground was a little wet but we sat on the big roots, which were dry. We all leaned our backs against the trunk. Teddy had a little bottle of peach schnapps and he passed it around. I asked if they wanted some of the joint I'd been smoking and we passed that around.

"That's pretty good shit," said Ivan.

"What do you think about that suicide?" I said.

"I think the parents made him do it," said Teddy.

"He *was* Asian," said Ivan. He was on the other side of Teddy and I couldn't see him.

"What does that mean?" I said.

"That they worked his ass like crazy and pressured the shit out of him."

"Do you think it hurt?" I said.

"For a second," said Teddy. "But if it's all going to be over anyway, then why does it matter? Pain only matters if it's pro-longed." Ivan was sucking long on the joint, then he said, "If I was going to kill myself, I wouldn't waste it. I would do a bunch of crazy shit first. Maybe kill some people I didn't like and take 'em with me."

We all thought about that. Then I said, "Wouldn't it be better to do a bunch of crazy *good* things before you died instead of killing people?"

"Like what?" said Teddy.

"I don't know. Give your life to save a bunch of kids or something."

"But that's what you're supposed to do every day, not if you're suicidal," he said. "If you're suicidal you're probably only thinking of yourself."

I drank the syrupy alcohol.

"I try to be good," I said.

"Me too," said Teddy.

"Fuck good people," said Ivan, and we laughed.

We finished the joint and I gave them both cigarettes. The stars were dots between the branches. On the other side of Teddy, Ivan started carving in the tree with a knife. He carved SUICIDE RULZ. Teddy was next and wrote FUCK GUNN. They told me I had to write something.

"I feel bad, the tree is so old."

"Fuck you," said Ivan. "Do it."

I drew a heart. It was hard to make it round because of the bark, so it was jagged on one side.

* * *

Eighth grade continued. For a month Mr. B acted like nothing happened. Our team was doing well and he just acted like a coach so I just acted like a player. But it was hard, because it was like I was just one of the other girls. He told his jokes to everyone but I didn't laugh as much.

Then on Halloween Mr. B asked me to trick-or-treat with him and Michael. I was surprised but I said okay. I dressed as a cat in black tights and Tiff drew whiskers on my face with black lipstick. Mr. B was dressed in a 49ers jersey and football pants and a helmet. He said he was supposed to be Steve Young. On the back of the jersey it said YOUNG and there was a big 8. Michael was dressed as Link, the elf from his video game. He wore green and had a little sword and a plastic jack-o'-lantern for candy.

We walked around and Michael would go up to each door and get candy and we would wait for him on the sidewalk. We talked a little about the soccer team. The championships were coming up and we were tied for first place with Mountain View.

He told me a joke: "A horse falls into a mud puddle and can't get out. So a chicken ties the horse to the bumper of his Mercedes and pulls him out. Later, the *chicken* falls into the mud, but the horse just stands close and says, 'Grab on to my thingy and pull yourself out.' The moral is, if you're hung like a horse you don't need a Mercedes to pick up chicks." I said it was funny, but I didn't laugh.

Later we went back to his place. He let Michael pick three candies to take to bed with him and made him leave the plastic jack-o'-lantern on the coffee table in the living room. While they were back in the bedroom I waited on the couch. I ate one of Michael's Baby Ruths and then I took a roll of Smarties. They were really sour so I just had two and put the rest in my sock with the Baby Ruth wrapper.

Mr. B came back out; he didn't have the helmet on. He sat on the couch and asked if I wanted any of Michael's candy. I said no.

"You're a very pretty cat."

"Why don't we talk at school anymore?"

"You know why."

"I know, but you could at least be nice to me. It's like you don't even like me anymore."

"Are you crazy? I'm in love with you, April."

I told him I had to go, that there was a party that the girls were having and I was late. I stood up, but he stood up too and grabbed my shoulders.

"Listen to me, I love you. Okay? I *love* you. I have just been weird because I didn't want anything bad to happen. But I don't care now. I want to be with you. We'll work it out. You can just come babysit all the time or something." He laughed a little and tried to get me to laugh by looking into my eyes and squeezing my shoulders. I pushed against him.

"I have to go."

"April, why? So you can hang around a bunch of little boys? Come on, you're better than that. Stay here, with me. We'll just watch a movie, I'm sure there is something scary and stupid on." I wanted to stay but I was feeling emotional. I pushed his hands away and left.

The next week our soccer team played in the championships. They were a week long at a junior high school called Egan in Los Altos. Mr. B seemed like he wanted to be nice but I stayed away from him and just played. On the last day we lost to Mountain View. When the team came out of the locker room Mr. B asked if anyone wanted a ride home. Shauna and Sandy said they did. He looked at me.

"April? Would you like a ride?" The other girls were looking at me so I said yes. In the car everyone was sad about losing so we didn't say much. He dropped Sandy off first because she lived in the nice part of town. He told her she had played very well.

When he dropped Shauna off he said, "You're the best team I've ever coached."

Then we drove. I was in the front seat. He wasn't driving toward my house but I didn't say anything. It was getting dark. "April, you really are the best player." I didn't say anything. "You want to hear a joke?" I didn't say anything so he didn't tell it. I took my cigarettes from my bag and I lit one. He didn't say anything but he cracked my window.

At his house he parked and told me that Michael was still at day care. He got out, and after a second I got out. Inside, he got me some water from the kitchen but I didn't drink it. I just kissed him. I did it hard because I was angry with him and sad because of the game. And sad because soccer was over and it was the thing I knew how to do best. We went to the couch. I was wearing sweats and he undressed me and got a condom and I lay on my back and we did it, simple. And then it was over. I was fourteen. We got dressed and he drove me home. At my house I saw the Smarties from Hal-

139

loween on my desk. I undid the plastic wrapper and ground each one into powder.

For the rest of the year, I went to Mr. B's all the time. Sometimes to babysit and sometimes not. We'd sit in his living room, in the dark, and watch TV. Most Saturdays we'd watch *Saturday Night Live,* and weekdays we'd watch reruns of *Cheers.* He had a good body, good hair, and a nice smile. He was funny; he liked television and funny movies. He wasn't older and I wasn't younger. We went to the mall sometimes too and got clothes. We always took Michael to the mall.

The next year I went to high school at Paly but I still went to Mr. B's all the time. My parents thought I was babysitting. I would tell Mr. B that I loved him and he would tell me. My sister was the only one who knew. She said it was okay as long as we were in love.

After everything had been going on with Mr. B for almost two years, I went to a party one night. I usually didn't go to parties because I spent so much time with Mr. B. I went with Shauna and Alice. They were my only friends and that was only because I saw them at soccer.

When we got to the house everyone was sitting around the living room; some were on the couch and some were on the carpet. The carpet was beige and so was the couch, and the walls were dark wood paneling. Everyone was being pretty quiet. The girls and I went to the kitchen and got some beers from some junior guys, Denny Johnson and Beau. I wanted to be like the other girls so I laughed when the guys said things.

Back in the main room, someone put on *Menace II Society,* so then everyone was sitting around the floor watching the big brown TV on the beige carpet. The movie was stupid. It tried too hard. It was trying to show a tough kind of life, but also be cool about it. There were shootings and sex and car jackings and everyone was too tough to care. I watched for an hour and drank three beers. After an hour I went outside to smoke.

Teddy was out there. There were a few other people off in the dark. I hadn't talked to him in a while because he was in the smart classes. I pulled out my pack of Reds, but it was empty. I asked Teddy for a cigarette. Teddy handed me a Camel Light. I lit it with my black lighter and tasted the difference. I saw Teddy's reflection and my reflection in the sliding glass door, and behind the reflections was everyone else inside, watching the movie.

"That's a stupid movie," I said. Teddy laughed and I could tell he was drunk. He asked me why I thought it was stupid. *"Because,"* I said. "We know the ghetto is bad, that's why it's the *ghetto,* but that movie is making it look cool. Like Ivan and all those guys are getting all excited about O-Dog because he shoots innocent people and laughs about it. That's not cool—the guy is a fucking murderer."

Teddy laughed again, then he said, "I like the part when the crack addict guy says, 'I'll suck ya dick.'"

"You like *that* part?"

"Yeah, it's funny because it's just like this part from *Boyz n the Hood,* where this woman crack addict says, 'I'll suck your dick'—it's like the exact same scene, but in *Menace* it's a *guy*

141

crack addict who says it. It's like they're trying to make the movie even crazier than *Boyz n the Hood* because a *guy* says 'I'll suck your dick.'"

"I guess," I said.

"And then O-Dog shoots the guy. He thinks the offer somehow makes *him* gay. And it's like the movie is saying gay people are the worst kind of people. Like even if everyone is living in a ghetto and it's hell, the gay person is the worst. Like a man sucking a dick is the most desperate you could get."

"Maybe," I said. "But why the hell would that make you like that scene?"

"I just mean I think it's funny, I don't *like* it."

"I just think it's a stupid movie," I said. "I think most movies and TV shows and video games are stupid."

"Okay," he said, and sucked his cigarette hard and then let out a big thing of smoke.

"You're crazy, right?" he said through the smoke. I said I wasn't and he said that I was.

"Why do you think I'm crazy?" I said.

He took another drag and said, "Because you don't care about anything."

"I *do* care," I said. "I care too much, but it never works. Like now—I'm trying to be here, I'm trying to do things. But it doesn't work, I can't find anything, so maybe that's what makes me crazy."

"What does that mean?"

"Nothing. I think *you* don't care about anything, Teddy, not me."

"I care about *you*," he said quietly, then he looked at me from the side of his face.

"Oh, shut up," I said. "You hardly even see me."

"Well I wish I did. I try to call you all the time, but you're always gone."

"I have soccer and shit," I said.

"I love you," he said. I laughed because he was drunk. But I could also tell that he was a little serious. I looked right at him and it was in that moment I knew it meant nothing to say that. I got very quiet and looked away and we sat staring at our reflections. Then I said, "You remember that night in eighth grade, after Shauna's bat mitzvah, we went to Gunn and sat under that tree? And I carved a heart in it?"

"Yeah."

"I wish we could go back to that night."

"Ivan and I cut it down."

"The *tree?*" I said. He nodded in the reflection and smoked. "You cut down the whole tree? It was huge."

"I know. One night last year we used his stepdad's saw. Just me and him. It took a long time. That thing was probably there since the Civil War. Now it's gone."

Sitting there with Teddy, I knew I was making a decision, but I didn't know what.

We smoked. The Camels weren't my brand but they were okay in the night air.

After that I stopped seeing Mr. B as often. He said I was being a baby. I told him I needed to spend more time with people my age, but when I wasn't with him I just ended up sitting in my room at home. Tiff wasn't even around. One night Mr. B asked me to babysit Michael because he had something important to do. I told him no.

"*Please*. He likes you, April."

"No he *doesn't*."

"Yes he *does*. If you don't do it for me, do it for him. He's used to having you around."

"Are you really going out?"

"Yes. I'd rather spend time with you, but I guess you won't let me."

I didn't even kiss Mr. B when he left. Michael was seven now. He may have been used to me, but he still didn't talk to me. He was in his regular position on the floor playing a game called Street Fighter. I sat on the couch and smoked.

"You're not supposed to smoke in here." I didn't answer. I ashed in my Diet Coke can and watched him fight different characters. After my cigarette I told him that I wanted to play. I sat on the floor next to him and picked up the other controller.

"You have to pick. Who do you want to be?"

"I want to be the girl."

"Chun Li? She sucks."

"I don't care, I want to be Chun Li." He told me what to press. "Now how do I fight you?"

"You press the buttons," he said. He was this Chinese guy and he beat the shit out of me. I pressed the buttons and my girl punched and kicked but it didn't do any good. He killed me twice and the game was over. "Two cookies," he said.

"What?"

"I get two cookies, I won."

"What are you talking about?"

"That's the rules."

"No it's not. Your dad said you get four cookies and you already had them."

"Cindy lets me."

"Who?"

"My other babysitter."

"Who is she?"

"She's my other babysitter. She lets me have cookies."

I stood up and walked to the kitchen. He was telling me he wanted one Oreo and one chocolate chip when I walked out the back door.

I didn't know where to go. I drove. Nirvana was in the CD player and I turned it off. I just drove and smoked. I didn't want to go home. I smoked four cigarettes. I had only one more left so I drove to 7-Eleven. I bought some more Reds with my sister's ID and a Diet Coke. Outside, I used the pay phone. First I called my sister, but she wasn't there. I called Shauna and then I called Alice. Alice said there was a party and gave me the address. I got in the car but I didn't turn the key. The lights inside the 7-Eleven made everything look yellow. The light fractured when I started crying.

After a while I started the car and drove slowly back toward Mr. B's. I had one more cigarette in the old pack. I had turned it upside down so I could make a wish. I put it in my mouth and lit it and made a desperate wish.

Tar Baby

This guy, A. J. Sims, and I, we got a bottle and drank it in his bedroom in the basement of his house. Vodka, clear and burning. We drank it straight from the big glass bottle.

A.J. had seven brothers, older and younger, so there were clothes, cups, and trash all over the house and some of the walls were flaking paint. There wasn't much space, and all A.J. had for privacy was this shitty little underground room with a bed two inches off the floor, and his boom box and his hip-hop mix tapes.

I was pretty drunk that night. We were listening to the Pharcyde. I was drinking much more than he was. I sat in the one chair by the desk and he sat on the bed.

A bubble came up from my stomach and burned my throat. It came out rank and when I swallowed it tasted like acid.

Just then, I don't know why, I said, "Oh, crap, A.J., fuck you." I laughed and my esophagus was burning.

A.J. looked up from his deep thoughts on the bed.

"Don't say that shit, bitch," he said, and he was not laughing.

"What shit?" I said.

"Fuck you, Teddy. Don't be sitting over there like a grinning baboon sayin' shit. I'll fuck you up." He wasn't really looking at me.

"Okay," I said, and drank some more from the bottle. It was a great bottle, really smooth. Smirnoff. I took a sip of tap water from a little orange plastic cup.

Then A.J. was up and pacing around the room. Three big steps in one direction, three steps back, over and over again. He was hunched over in a white T-shirt that was grayed from washing, and his wiry forearms were flexing and unflexing.

He had moved to Palo Alto from LA the year before, so he thought he had a reputation to maintain. He was just a skinny little guy with a bowling ball head, but he arrived talking big. For a while he got a bit of respect because he wrote good graffiti and claimed that he liked big black asses. His tag was "Icer" for some reason, and then he changed it to "Ajay" because it was like his name but spelled differently. He always drank a lot of pineapple juice to make his come taste good. "Like cocoa butter," he said.

Three months after his arrival, he was a joke. Everyone saw he was actually psycho. As soon as he got drunk he would do stupid things like put cigarettes out on his arms or ride his scooter into a wall. And he would talk even bigger when he was drunk. He'd say, "Nigger." One night he said the wrong thing to some of the black guys and got beat up. He wasn't so tough after that. He was alone a lot. That's when he started doing weird things even when he wasn't drunk, like doing the cigarette burns at school. He really had no friends. Except me. He was a little bald weirdo, with burns up his forearm like leopard spots.

It was ten o'clock and I was staring at the tape turning in the boom box. Little gears rotating. The Geto Boys were talking about dick sucking, and licking scrotums and assholes. A.J. was back on the low bed with the ratty blue blanket and he was making a call.

"Yo, shut up for a minute, I'm calling April," he said. "Turn that shit down."

I turned the music off. We sat there while he waited. A long depressing quiet as the phone rang.

April was in our class, but she was better than us, mature and experienced. She had an older sister, and she'd introduced her to a lot. When April showed up in our town from Arizona at age thirteen with her tan and muscular legs, she had already fucked. She knew about dicks and talked about them to us in whispers. She knew that some bent in funny ways.

I had a crush on April right away. In eighth grade I called her once and tried to act cool. At least she was nice. She lived near me and sometimes we would go to the park near her house and sit on the swings and smoke pot out of her little pink pipe. After we got into high school she started fucking older guys. This guy Denny Johnson and this guy Adam Cohen. They played water polo, and were really tall. Also my friend Barry.

Then A.J. was on the phone with her. He was smiling. I sat in the chair and cursed him in my mind.

"You should meet us," A.J. said into the white phone. Then he was listening very intensely. He wasn't such a gangster then; he was just a sweetie.

". . . well bring your sister with you. It will be cool," he said. He was looking at me like he was making sure I wasn't laughing at him. She was saying something because I could hear the little buzz in the phone.

". . . then bring your sister *and* Emily too."

I was warm and drunk. Inside, I felt things flow through me and I thought about cartoon rabbits and about William Faulkner and how he drank all the time. I thought that someday I would be him.

When I was a baby, my mom read to me from Uncle Remus. I thought about the Tar Baby, his body steaming, just after Br'er Fox pulled him out of the cooking pot. A raw, coal-dark coagulum that Br'er Fox shaped into a slick black, shining, seal-like thing. A little black podling. No face until Br'er Fox pulled off Br'er Bear's two jacket buttons and stuck them on the black baby and those were the eyes.

Button eyes are a crazy man's eyes.

> *Buggedy* bu*ggedy* bu*ggedy boo,*
> *I have crazy eyes, how about you?*

A.J. looked away and listened. I couldn't believe April was talking to A.J.

"No, Teddy is here. Yes, *Teddy,*" said A.J. into the phone. Then he turned to me. "She says hi."

"Hi, April," I said, but he didn't relay the message. He was facing the wall again.

"Yeah, he's all drunk," he said. "He can hang out with Emily."

"Emily" was Emily Kraft, a big slut. She was a year older than us.

A.J. said, "Come on," five times in five different ways, like she was teetering on an edge and he was gently trying to blow her over. Finally he said, "At Addison," and his voice went a little higher. Addison was an elementary school down the street from his house.

"We'll be on the jungle gym," he said to the phone. He was smiling but not at me. The little guy had actually convinced them to come over. ". . . yeah, we got d'vodka . . . cool, see ya in the school yard, peace." He said "school yard" like he was singing a song.

After he hung up he stopped smiling and didn't share any of the joy. "They down," he said, real serious.

"*'D'* vodka'?" I said.

"Yeah, we got *d'vodka,* motherfucker, you got a problem wit that?"

"No," I said. "I'm glad we got it."

He was putting his jacket on. It was a Carhartt jacket, real plain. I had a brown corduroy one with a fur collar from J.Crew. I took it off the back of the chair. Some guy on a TV show had one too.

A.J. reached across me and took the bottle and screwed the cap on.

"You've been drinking this like a motherfucker," he said.

He tucked the large bottle under his jacket and it bulged.

"Let's go, bitch," he said.

A few of the brothers were shifting around in shadowy corners of the basement level, and when we walked upstairs there were some more sitting and lying on the floor in front of the TV. They were watching *Ace Ventura: Pet Detective*. I saw a little grape juice, deep purple and luminescent, at the bottom of a plastic glass.

Outside, it was a little cold, and the sound vacuumed out to quiet, nothing but a few cars passing in the distance along Middlefield Road. We went through the chain-link gate into the dark school yard. I sat on the end of the slide and the metal was cold under my ass. A.J. stood in the tanbark and paced a little; the bulge was still under his arm. Then we waited.

After five minutes I said, "Lemme get some of d'vodka." I was surprised but he reached under his jacket and handed the bottle to me. He put his hands in his jacket pockets and looked all around, alert but cool.

I unscrewed the red cap and tilted the bottle to my lips. The stuff went down and I pictured the clear liquid with a magical pink inner glow.

"Save some of that shit," A.J. said. A few cars passed but not the girls. I drank from the bottle again and it was a scary plunge because I always wanted to take too much. It hurt, but it was also impressive, like being in the hands of a bigger force. And because of that, a relief. A.J. still wasn't looking at me so I took another sip and my throat burned sharp and my brain swam in cold water.

A long silver-blue Cadillac passed, going very slowly. How we must look to adults: shitty teenagers in brown jackets, hanging around the school yard in the dark.

I thought again about the Tar Baby from Uncle Remus. The Tar Baby and the briar patch and Br'er Rabbit and Br'er Bear and Br'er Fox. I could probably get A.J. to fuck the Tar Baby if I made it look like a girl. Get his dick stuck in the tar. A.J. was so lonely and angry, and all his feelings got computed in strange ways. He said he had had a girlfriend in LA, a black girl. She must have hated herself. April was white, but A.J. really liked her.

After thirty minutes April and the girls weren't there. It was just us, cold in the cold.

A.J. had walked out of the tanbark onto the blacktop, and I was alone with the vodka for a while, but then he came back and started yelling.

"Save that shit for the girls, motherfuck!" he said, grabbing the bottle. He saw how much was left and yelled some more. I just sat there. He said, "You faggot ass, you shit-kissing motherfucker, you dumb fucking nigger, you shitfaced faggot, I oughtta kill you. . . ." Other stuff poured out, like he was talking to himself.

Some teenage girls walked by. They didn't go to our high school. There was a big-boned girl with short curly hair to her ears and a skinny witchy girl with longer black hair. They stood in the gateway.

"What are you yelling at?" said the big-boned girl. She said it like she was older than she was. She must have been lonely if she was bothering with us.

A.J. answered her like he had been expecting them. "This faggot doesn't know how to get any pussy, and drinks all my shit."

The girls laughed a little.

"Really? He doesn't know how to get any pussy?" said the big-boned girl.

"What an asshole," said the witchy one. She was talking about A.J.

Then I spoke up. It was the first chance I'd had after the yelling.

"You're the one who doesn't know how to get girls," I said to A.J.'s back. My words came out damp and wobbly.

A.J. whipped around for a second. Then he knew we were all against him. He was sensitive to that kind of thing. He whipped back to the girls.

"What the fuck do you bitches want?" A.J. said to the girls.

The big-boned girl had bangs and a nice smile and I liked her face. She had a fur-lined hooded jacket that I also liked, and I guessed maybe we would have been friends if we'd been somewhere else.

"We just wanted to see if you would give us a drink from your bottle," said the big-boned girl. The witchy girl was looking at the black sky.

"You're not getting any of this shit," said A.J., holding the bottle to his chest.

"Okay, fine," said the big-boned girl. There was one light on the back corner of the school building and some of it hit her mouth. I thought of a watermelon Jolly Rancher. Her lips were not a fat girl's lips; they were thin, and very juicy pink-red. But she was smiling a little funny, only on one side, like she wasn't sure if she should smile, and that was because A.J. was looking at her.

Then her lips were not in the light anymore because A.J. was moving toward the girls.

"Get the fuck out of here, bitches!" he said, waving the bottle. "We got some *fine* bitches coming, we don't need fat-ass and skinny!"

"Fuck you, asshole," said the big-boned one.

"Fuck you, you creepy little monkey," said the witchy one. The girls kept yelling at A.J. as they backed away into the dark. Then it was quiet.

When A.J. came back, there was nothing to say. And nothing to do because he was holding the bottle. I was feeling okay; I'd had enough vodka.

This was the way the night had cashed in. Choices had been made and things happened, and here we were. It was sad and funny. My life was made of this. Stuff like this.

I thought about how Br'er Bear walked around with a nail sticking out of his club. When I was eleven, I hammered a nail into a baseball bat. It was very dangerous. I made other weapons. And when my camp went on a field trip to Chinatown, I bought a throwing star. I thought I needed all those weapons, and I hoarded them.

I used to throw the star at the fence in the backyard, and it would stick in. I threw it at the cat, Stoney.

When I was twelve I took karate at the YMCA. We

learned katas and punches. I learned the katas really well. If you learned the katas, you got the higher belts. The order: white, yellow, orange, blue, green, brown, black. I was happy until I started fighting in school and the katas didn't do shit for me.

A.J. was in such a bad mood compared to me, but I couldn't help but laugh at him.

"Better shut up, clown," he said.

" 'We don't *need* fat-ass and skinny!' Ha-ha, you're fuckin' *funny*, A.J."

"Shut *up,* clown," he said, and kicked some of the tanbark at me but it fell short. I was still laughing.

"Cocoa *butter*!" I yelled. " 'My shit tastes like *cocoa butter*!' " A.J. grabbed my fur collar and yanked it back and forth, like he was going to shake the laugh out of me, but I was still laughing.

"Shut the fuck up, Teddy, or I swear to God, I'm-a fuck you up."

He yanked me up by the collar. "Get the fuck up," he said, and I was on my feet, but my head was going everywhere. "We're going to Ofra's."

"Ofra's?" He was already walking away from me with the bottle. I followed him out the gate and back across the street toward his house. His green Karmann Ghia was parked on the street. We got in. Funny old-fashioned interior with hard plastic seats.

Then we were driving and I was laughing again. A.J. looked

so serious I couldn't stop for a long while. When he finally spoke he was very quiet.

"All the clowns in the car better shut up," he said. He was still looking out the windshield. I had my feet up on the dash and no seat belt, and when he said that I laughed harder.

"*This* clown is *shut* up," I said. "What about the other ones?" And I cracked myself up some more. A.J. was driving really fast now.

Ofra Isaac was a girl in our class and she was having a party that night. She had a huge house in the nicest part of town. The funny thing about the nicest part of town was that it was the closest to East Palo Alto. There were all these mansions and then right down the road it was really bad. Kids would go over there to buy liquor and drugs, but a lot of the time they got into fights or got mugged. East Palo Alto was primarily black and Pacific Islander.

Ofra had a lot of parties at her house. Her parents didn't care. The problem was that Ofra didn't like me anymore, mostly because I got drunk all the time. The last time I was at her house me and my friend Ivan got in a fight. We stepped all over her white couch with our shoes and somehow we knocked the mezuzah off the front doorpost. Eventually we stopped fighting in her driveway, but Ofra wouldn't let us back in.

"You don't want to go to Ofra's," I said to A.J.

He didn't say anything. I looked around for the bottle, but he must have hid it in the back. Nothing was funny anymore.

"What do you think, A.J.?" I said. "That April is waiting

for you at Ofra's? That you're going to hook up with that ass?" His jaw flexed. "April *hates* you, A.J. *Everyone* hates you."

It was about eleven o'clock and the cool air from outside was coming in steady through the old Karmann Ghia hinges.

"Okay, A.J. A.J. dog. One question. That's it, that's all you got to answer, one question, and then you can be done with me. You can throw me out of this car if you want." He said nothing, just drove very fast, which was scary around the corners. "Okay, here it is. So what do you think you'll be doing in twenty years? No, make it easier, *ten* years. What will you be doing?"

It was like he didn't hear me, but he did.

"Rapping?" I said. "Are you going to be a rapper?"

No answer.

"Writing graffiti? Married? Maybe have a bunch of kids? With April? You think you and April are gonna have a million kids like your parents?"

A.J. braked the car really fast. So fast that my knees hit the metal dash and the back of the car started sliding. Then we were stopped. He reached across me and opened the passenger door, and then he had his back braced against his door and he was kicking me out the door. I was laughing, except not too much because his kicks hurt and I was trying to stop because A.J. was crying.

"Get the fuck out, get out, get out!" Then my ass hit the ground and I was outside in some grass and the cold air. A.J. drove off. He stopped a few yards away, reached across the seat, and slammed the passenger door. The green hump of the Karmann Ghia got smaller and smaller and then he was gone.

A paint marker that A.J. used for graffiti had fallen out

with me. It had a purple cap and a purple body and on the side it said SOLID MARKER. I sat in the long grass between the sidewalk and the street, and when I took the cap off I saw that the paint stick was two colors: yellow and purple. A.J. had cut the purple paint stick in half and fused it with half a yellow paint stick so that the colors would swirl together. I put the stick in my pants pocket.

I was close to Jordan, my old middle school, where I first met April. I went over there. The lights in the roof of the outdoor halls were on. Some of the old feelings came back, some faces flashed, all things I didn't like. I drew some large monsterlike baby faces on the walls and wrote FUCK ALL BITCHES LIKE APRIL SPARK in bad graffiti script. I had practiced graffiti writing a lot but I was never going to be as good as A.J., and I was really drunk. Next to one of the large baby monsters I wrote LOVE, A.J. SIMS NIGGA.

Then I walked out of the school yard toward Ofra Isaac's house.

Ofra's was pretty far away.

After a while, I saw an old man walking a little white dog. He had a full head of nicely combed white hair. I caught up to him even though I was stumbling a little.

"Hey. Hey, man . . . ," I said, in a friendly tone. But the guy didn't stop. He didn't look at me, even though I was just a little behind him.

"I'm a really nice guy," I said, but he walked faster. "I just want some company and you seem like a nice guy too." I talked to him like that for a few blocks without him answering or looking back. I kept following him even though it was out of my way to get to Ofra's. I wanted to convince this guy that I was a good person. Then he turned into a house.

"You better get the fuck out of here," he said. "I'm calling the police, you fucking asshole." Then he went inside. I left.

I was walking, back on track for Ofra's. I walked with my head bowed so I could watch my feet.

I started thinking about Jack Kerouac and what a hero he was. "You're a hero," I said out loud. "Like Jack Kerouac." I liked thinking about Kerouac stumbling around drunk.

Then I happened upon another guy. He was old too, with a slightly bigger, brown dog. He was taller than the first guy. He wore an Irish cap and was a little more disheveled. When I tried to pass him, he said, "Hey," and smiled.

"What's up?" I said.

"Nothing, just walking my dog."

"I'm not here to mug you or anything," I said, because of the other guy being so scared.

"I know," he said.

"Can I walk with you?"

"Sure," he said, and we walked.

"I've been fighting with my girlfriend," the old guy said. "She won't give me any head."

"That sucks," I said.

"You have a girl?"

"No. Fuck girls," I said.

"Yeah. Fuck 'em," he said.

"Fuck guys too."

We walked without talking for a bit.

Then he said, "When I was young, I was really angry and

shy. I'd do stupid stuff like steal and set fires. I never got caught. Now I'm old and I feel the same way. You know what I mean? I don't *like* anything."

"Sure," I said.

"Is that how *you* feel?"

"Yeah, I hate everything," I said.

We walked past a church. I had read Ibsen's *Ghosts* in the parking lot one day while waiting for an AA meeting because the court made me go.

"I'm really not here to mug you," I said.

He didn't say anything.

I said, "You want to frisk me?"

"Yeah," he said, like it was a regular thing. So we stepped off the sidewalk and through the edge of the church parking lot to the brick side of the chapel. We were behind a large juniper bush, hidden from the road. I put my hands on the bricks like I was being arrested and he frisked me. He touched me under my arms and on my sides and on my butt a little. Then he was done.

"Okay?" I said.

"Can I feel your balls for a second?"

"What? What the fuck?"

"Come on, man, be cool and just let me feel your balls for a second."

"Aw, man," I said. "I was trying to be nice to make you feel safe and you pull that shit?"

"I'm sorry," he said.

We walked out of the church and along the sidewalk, and we didn't talk anymore.

A car full of teenagers drove by and yelled to us. I didn't know them but I wanted to be with them. They were stopped at a light at Embarcadero. I ran up to the car and asked to be let in, but they wouldn't open the door. When the light turned green the car started moving, but I held on to the open window and ran alongside. The girls inside were shrieking. It was like they were scared but excited too. The car went faster and then I was falling and I slid on the street on my back. The car drove off and when I stood up the old man with the dog was gone.

I walked past a bunch of houses. I was coming up on another elementary school called Duvenek and I knew that meant I was close to Ofra's. I climbed the chain-link fence and crossed the wet grass field. I passed through the outdoor halls and drew a few purple and yellow flowers for the kids. Then I wrote FUCK SCHOOL.

Outside the school there was one more street to go and then I was at Ofra's. When I got to the mouth of her drive-way I could hear the buzzing voices of the party. People were probably around the pool in the back, and April and her sister and Emily were probably there too. I was sure A.J. wasn't.

I didn't go in. I walked down the wide street with all the mansions. The mansions ended and the street started to nar-row. Soon there was thick foliage on both sides and the side-walk ended. I walked over a small arched bridge and there I was, in East Palo Alto.

It was darker over here. Fewer streetlights. The houses were slanted and there were metal bars in front of the win-dows.

I was mad at everyone but there was nothing I could do.

I started yelling. First it was just screaming, no words.

When cars passed, I yelled at them, "Hey! Take me! Take me! Take me out of here! Take me with you."

I yelled at every car that passed. Nobody stopped.

Ten minutes later a cop car drove up and took me away.

You can't fight the Tar Baby, that's what he *wants*. You punch that Tar Baby and he sucks you in. Once you get wrapped up with the Tar Baby, he loses his shape, he becomes a sticky, black goo-monster and he gets all over you. The more you fight, and stretch him, and struggle, the more he gets all over you, and then you can't move and you're just a pile of tar. After a certain point, you are the Tar Baby. Instead of button eyes, you still have your real eyes, looking out from under the tar.

I Could Kill Someone

There are many ways to kill someone, but a gun seems as good as any. The big thing that gets you caught is motive. It's pretty obvious that Brent Baucher hates me, but who would expect me to get a gun and kill him?

He's on the football team. He is not handsome. He's fit, but he's a beast, very hairy arms and legs: strong, pale, discolored things.

I'm told that I am good-looking, but I hate my body, and my face, and my curly hair. And I'm shy.

Brent has a large bulging forehead that makes his eyes sit deep in his skull. The bottom of his face is too long, like it was squeezed in a vise. There are white-capped acne bulges, pink and irritated. And single hairs coming out of strange areas.

In World History I once saw him doodling on a returned exam. Next to the red *F* at the top he wrote "uck 'em all." Then under that he wrote "Niggas Unite." Then he scribbled out his last name and wrote "Too $hort," like the rapper.

I'd like to take Brent out of reality, just as simple as leading him through a door.

I don't like violence. I don't play video games, and I don't go to horror movies. I like *Steel Magnolias*; I like Sally Field.

One time, in my sophomore year, I had to stay after school and run around the track because I had been late to Mr. Peterson's PE class twenty times in a row. That gray afternoon, going around, I thought about the oval of the track, and the rectangle of the football field within it, and the smaller rectangles of the field defining the yard lines. The memory of all those circles and rectangles is tied up with what happened later in the locker room.

When I got in from the track, the last of the football team was in there changing after practice. I walked to the far bank of lockers, along the wall, where my locker was. I could hear them cavorting and laughing, and as I walked I could see out of my peripheral vision that one of the five or six of them was Brent Baucher.

I sat on the wooden bench and swirled the black dial back and forth, and behind me, in the center aisle, the five and Brent erupted in laughter. The sound bounced around the cement room. That laughter had been in that place forever; it was something that those boys had found when they got to high school.

"You looked, motherfucker! Faggot looked!"

"Cecil looked! Faggot looked!"

"No I din'n," said Cecil's voice, but it was drowned in laughter and the sounds of bodies moving around.

I changed as fast as I could, my shirt first and then quickly off with my shorts and on with my jeans.

Then I realized that the locker room was very quiet, and when I looked over my shoulder the six of them were standing in their underwear and they were all still muddy and dirty and covered in grass, and I saw Baucher's chest in a tight white tank, hair sprouting everywhere, and then I noticed something that made my mind jump; they each had one testicle sticking out of the pee hole in the front of their underpants; endless balls, pulled tight against scrotum skin; pink, brown, and paste. For a flash of a second, I saw Brent's: large, kidney shaped, blue veined, and hairy.

I looked up and saw their faces and I knew I was not supposed to be looking at those balls, that that was what they wanted.

"Faggot looked!" said someone. And then they all said it, while they tucked in their balls and moved toward me. They screamed that I was a faggot as two held me down. One sat on my face—Cecil, I think; his crotch smelled sour and rich, and his balls in their cloth sack were on my chin. Down below, the others pulled my jeans off and my underwear. Someone grabbed my balls and twisted. At first it felt like a bubble in my stomach that went up to my throat and filled it, like my balls were up there and choking me, and then they twisted further, and the skin of my scrotum burned as it twisted and chafed against itself.

"Again!" someone yelled.

"Again!" another person yelled. They were all yelling "Faggot" again, and my balls were twisting again, and before I started screaming into the white wall of Cecil's underwear, and biting at the chalky brown of his inner thigh, I realized that I could not hear Brent's voice in all the yelling. Before things went black I realized that Brent's silence meant that he was doing the twisting.

Brent is very stupid. He gets all Ds and Fs in his classes. I have World History with him; he said that the Black Plague was started by a combination of gays and rats. We studied the French Revolution in that class. One time, I masturbated to David's painting of Marat. It was a picture in my textbook, and I let the come go right in there, and then I closed it. Now the pages are cemented together, and dead Marat is plastered against the guillotine forever.

This is Brent's joke: "What's the difference between a faggot and shit?" I didn't know the answer. "Nothing, you fucking *faggot*." He told that joke one time, and then kicked my foot to trip me into dog shit on the quad lawn. I didn't fall, but everyone thought it was funny.

Brent says I'm a faggot because I quit the football team freshman year. I asked him about it and that's when we had our first little scene.

"You think I'm a fag because I quit the team?" I said.

He stopped. He had his usual black San Diego Chargers hat on backward. His long face looked surprised, and the one stoned-looking eye opened a little bit more.

"You *are* a fucking fag," he said. He looked like he was getting a little emotional about it. I could see it in his retarded eyes.

"Why do you think that?" I said, and my voice trembled.

"I don't *think* it, you are!" Then he walked off. It's weird, but I think it's because he was going to cry. After that he always called me a faggot.

After the locker room I decided that Brent needed to die. He was never going to get smarter, and he was a bigot. And I couldn't stop thinking about his acne-corroded flesh being opened, and his thin racist blood matting the hair of his beastly body.

I was standing over near the underpass next to the school where people smoked. Some people called it the Bat Cave.

"You really want one?" said Barry. Barry was my friend. He was chubby and lovable, and Mormon, and smoked pot and loved John Bonham.

"Yes," I said. "I want one."

I wanted a gun.

Barry couldn't get me one, but he knew a guy who could.

"Sheeze, well, okay, but . . . sheeze, all right, I have to talk to Teague."

Teague went to Menlo, a private school in the next town. Teague was infamous. Barry knew him because Barry went to Menlo in eighth grade.

Teague was dating a girl named Kate Keller who went to the all-girls school, Castilleja. My mom used to teach there. Kate and Teague fucked all the time, so people said. One time, Barry told me that in eighth grade Teague took Kate to *Wayne's World* and fingered her during the whole movie. Just watching and working.

Everyone knew that Teague could get guns.

Two days later, on Thursday, Barry came up to me in the cafeteria at brunch. I was in the food line. Barry put his face close to mine, but he wasn't looking at me. He whispered, "Here it is."

I looked right at him, but he was looking at the back wall, like he was pretending he wasn't talking to me.

"What?" I whispered at his big Mormon ear.

"T's number."

While he said that he was putting a piece of paper in my hand.

"Don't look now," he whispered. He still wasn't looking at me.

"Okay," I said. "Thanks." And I put the note in my jacket pocket.

Then it was my turn to order at the food window. I stepped up and said to the woman in the hairnet, "Hi, Ann, can I have some Tater Tots and a Diet Coke?"

While Ann was getting my Tots, Barry stepped over to me again. This time he was looking me in the eyes.

"Don't do anything stupid," he said.

"I won't," I said. I made sure I was looking right back at his eyes.

He looked at me like he was trying to determine something, but I doubt that he could.

Then he said, "You coming to Battle of the Bands?"

"Yeah," I said.

At lunch that day I sat with some people, but I didn't listen to them talk. I kept feeling the crumpled paper in my pocket.

In math class I sat in the back. It was AP Calculus, and I was the youngest in the class. Mr. Case was large and dark and bald. He was the assistant football coach under Coach Peterson, the cock. He looked so thick, like hardened tree sap; his eyes were a little crossed and he had a lazier left eyelid than Brent Baucher. He lived three hours away in a place called Angels Camp, on the way to Lake Tahoe.

Mr. Case drove three hours each morning to be at school, and then drove back after football practice to be with the angels.

I was good at math, but not as good as others. My dad forced me into it, so I had no love for it. I tried to think of the equations on the blackboard like little winking eyes and explosions the way Stephen Dedalus did, but it all just looked like a bunch of work that I didn't want to do.

I fingered the paper in my pocket, and then I pulled it out. I unfolded it and it was the ripped corner of Barry's English handout. The typed homework part of it said, ". . . what does George do after Lenny dies? Write a different ending that . . . ," but the rest was ripped off, and underneath that, Barry had written "T" for Teague, but the *T* was slanted and it looked like an *X*. Underneath the *T* was the phone number, written in a scraggly and uneven hand.

There were three nines in Teague's number and two twos.

After school I sat at a picnic bench and read some Faulkner until about five. Benjy was so retarded, and I loved Quentin. I wanted to stick a knife in my throat, or fuck my sister if I had one, and then jump off a bridge at Harvard. I thought about it for a while, then I called Teague's number from the pay phone at school.

The number went to a pager, so I paged it to the pay phone. I stood there and waited. Cars drove by on El Camino. No one in those cars knew what was going on over here, on the school campus. A little ways away, in the locker room on the other side of campus, Brent was probably changing, or playing Faggot Looked. Funny that he had no idea what I was doing so close to him.

The pay phone rang after five minutes.

"Hello?" the voice said. The voice was nasal, and it sounded angry, but like a teenager's.

"Hey, it's Teddy," I said. "Barry C. gave me this number."

The voice changed a little. "Hey. Yeah, he told me. So you need that thing?"

"Uh, yeah."

"Yeah, I can help you." The voice was really relaxed now. It sounded like he was doing something on the other end, like rolling marbles on a table, one by one. Then he said, "Can you meet me Saturday night?"

I told him that was okay. Ordering a gun was like ordering anything, it turned out.

He said we should meet at Cubberley, this closed high school, at midnight on Saturday. I said okay, and then we hung up.

I took my sweatshirt sleeve and rubbed the fingerprints off the phone receiver. And then I ran.

I couldn't sleep that night. It was like Christmas Eve, but not. It was something dark. I wasn't going to get or give anything; I was just going to take something away.

The next day was Friday. I was very tired, and I felt like everyone could see the gun shining in my mind, and there were bright flashing words above it that read BRENT BAUCHER.

I sat in Biology and thought about Brent. Protozoa had cilia like the hairs on Brent's legs. Brent's cells had all his information coiled into DNA, in every one of those dirty nuclei. I wanted to destroy those cells. Break 'em up like billiard balls and have all that info obliterated. His mitochondrial forehead and his Golgi vesicle pimples, and his dead, void mind, shut down and gone.

Then, after Biology and before English, I passed Brent in the outdoor breezeway.

It was a shock because I had been thinking about him so intensely right before, but it was also a shock because I usually didn't pass him in the halls. I was usually sure to take routes that kept me away from him.

"What's up, little bitch?" he said.

I wasn't smaller than him, I was just weaker. "Fuck you, little bitch," I said back. But I said it quietly into my shoulder, and after he passed.

But then, behind me, he said, "Did you say something?"

I stopped and turned, and he was walking right at me. I started backing away.

"Did you say something, faggot?" he said.

Then I put my hands in front of my face, but he got through them with his fist, and hit me. I felt his knuckle connect with my cheekbone, sharp. And then I fell, because I was surprised, and because I tripped over a bush.

I was on the ground, and there were a few people watching from far away, but no one came over.

"You are going to be dead before you know it," I said.

I was surprised I had said that, but I didn't show that I was surprised.

Brent looked surprised too; his droopy eye opened a little more, and then it went down again and he got evil.

"Are you fucking *high* right now, faggot?" he said, leaning over me. I was holding my cheek, and maybe even crying a little. I had fallen in an area for plants; there was sharp tanbark under my hand and some shitty juniper bushes.

The people in the distance were just standing and watching.

Then I got loud through my tears. "I'm high on how fucking stupid you are!" I said. "I mean, you are soooo dumb, Too $hort! Brent too short, too dumb, too many pimples, shitface! What a fucking idiot!" I started laughing up at his face. The gun was giving me power, even though I didn't have it yet. "Ha-ha-ha-ha-ha," I laughed. "It's, like, why aren't you dead yet?"

Brent's dumb face just looked so stupid at that point, and it looked like he was trying to straighten his left eyeball, under the lazy lid, but that he just couldn't, and I laughed even more because it was twitching. "Hey, twitchy eye, why don't you just die of being a fucking shitbag?"

I thought this was a pretty good line.

Brent reached down for the front of my shirt, but I curled up into a ball, so he couldn't grab me. He roared like a boar, long and angry, and then he started stomping on my ribs. Quick, hard stomps. My ribs bent, and my lungs were jolted, and there was a sucking-in sound. I stayed rolled up and he stomped me. Then there were some shouts from afar, and Brent was gone.

On Saturday night I went to get the gun.

Cubberley was a high school that had been shut down two decades before. It was famous because some of the Grateful

Dead had gone there forty years ago, but now it was a big empty campus where adult classes met and where children's sports teams played on the weekends. There were weeds in all the cracks of the arcade floors, and dead vines on the walls. I had been forced to play a lot of sports there when I was younger, so I knew the place well.

I rode my bike there because I was too young to drive. It was about four miles from my house. Teague and I were supposed to meet at the outdoor auditorium. I rode fast and the cold air on my face felt like I was riding through ghosts.

When I got to the school, I walked my bike down the hallway. On the walls, there were light fixtures every so often, which shone faint orange behind thick rippled plastic. They still kept the lights on every night, lighting nothing, for no one.

I walked past the gym, where I had played basketball when I was ten. The double doors had a chain through the handles, and there was a padlock hanging in the center. I had a memory flash of being small, in an oversized jersey, playing badly and hating myself. Then I was at the outdoor theater.

It had a stone stage and a grassy area for the audience. I was at the lip of the grassy part, at the far end from the stage. The moon lit up the place.

I left my bike at the edge of the grass and walked down the small declination toward the stage. The grass came up in uneven patches, and the dew soaked through the top of my black Converses, and through my socks to my feet.

* * *

I couldn't see anyone.

I thought about Brent coming out from the dark and shooting me.

If he knew I wanted to kill him, he would kill me first.

In the old days, you could duel.

Emotions have been around forever.

I wish I had a girlfriend. Or someone.

There was no one. I was in the middle of the grassy area. The stage was there, with its jagged lip of broken stone, looking spiritual in the moonlight.

I felt that weight on me, the weight of stone, and it was familiar. I was weak, and stupid, and wimpy, and I had no opinions, and I was a bad talker, and I didn't know how to make friends, and I had big ears, and an ugly nose, and my hair was 'fro-y, and my dick, and my stomach, and my mind were all bad.

But then a weird thing happened. While I stood there and waited for my gun, Brent changed a little in my mind. For a second, it seemed like he was just another guy. Brent was ugly, and he had human needs, and he probably had a bunch of disappointments in life. I suppose being so close to the gun, almost having it, made me think about things in a new way. Brent had problems, and he had skin, and he had a mom, and one day he would die too.

If I shot him, it wouldn't really matter. There would be

more people like him. Deer get shot all the time. Deer blood and deer guts all over the forest floor. Blood in the leaves, breathing slowing down. And then gone.

Brent would be forgotten too.

"Hey."

I turned. There was someone standing in a little alcove in the sidewall of the theater.

He had been watching me. It was Teague. There was cement behind him and above him and he was in shadow so it was hard to see his eyes.

There was another guy on the cement above us, but I couldn't really see him. I could only tell that he was big and white.

Teague was my height, and handsome. He wore a black parka but I could tell that he was skinny from his face and neck. He had curly brown hair cut pretty short.

He looked like he was about to laugh, but he didn't laugh, and because I couldn't really see his eyes, I was confused about what he was feeling. Maybe nothing.

"Here's the shit," said Teague, and he handed me a wrinkled paper bag. He didn't stop looking at me while I took the bag.

The bag was heavy. I looked inside, and there was a black handgun at the bottom.

"Take it out," he said.

"Nah, I'm cool," I said. "Looks good."

"You don't want to check it out?" he said.

"Nah, we're good," I said. "Three fifty-seven, right?"

"It's a Glock," he said. There was a sound from above, like scraping.

"I thought you said a three fifty-seven?"

"Glock's better," he said.

"Right, cool," I said.

"Three-hun," he told me.

"Oh, right." I took out a folded envelope from my back pocket and handed it to him. I had been saving for a car.

He counted the money and then put it in his back pocket.

"Nice doing business with you," he said, and walked out. He met his friend at the end of the grass, and they turned the corner down the hall with the orange lights and were gone.

The bag just looked like a lunch bag, so I carried it casually. I rode my bike home, and the bag swung under my handlebars. I was humming a little bit. Some tune. I saw my hand on my handlebars, gripping the handgrip and the top of the bag. I stopped humming and heard the air all around me, and my bike whirring below.

And you know how you can't see your face? The closest you can see is the tip of your nose, if you cross your eyes. But I wanted to look at myself right then, to see this guy coasting down the sidewalk with a gun, going somewhere.

Then the bag split and the gun clattered onto the cement. I skidded to a stop and turned around to get it. It was lying on the sidewalk in front of someone's lawn. A black gun on the sidewalk. It wasn't metal. It was plastic. It was a squirt gun, full of water. For a second I was sure of it, but no, it was a real gun. I picked it up. I didn't know how to check if it was okay. There was a button on the side of the grip that I pressed and the clip popped out in my hand. It was heavy and full of bullets.

I popped the clip back in.

Then I pointed the gun at the house I was in front of. It was an Eichler house, low and boxy, with a garage door out front—like my house, but orange and white. I pulled the trigger, and the gun fired. There was a loud burst and then the house was there, but even more there because it had just been shot.

A neighbor's dog barked, and I took off on my bike with the gun clutched to my chest.

Two weeks later was the Battle of the Bands. There were seven local bands from the various high schools, and I thought it was funny and fitting that it was in the gym at Cubberley.

I went to hear my friend Barry play. Barry was in a band called Headless Tom, I guess after Washington Irving and Mark Twain. Barry's brother was in the band, with two other pothead Mormons.

Most of the kids there were the alternative crowd from my school and other schools, but there were some jocks there too.

I stood to the side and watched. The gun was heavy in my jacket pocket.

Barry's band went on third.

Their first song was called "The Quick and the Dead," because those are the last words in the Mormon Bible. It is a song about friends who have died.

Across the pit I saw Teague swaying like a stalk of wheat. He looked like he was laughing, but I knew that he wasn't.

Then I saw Brent Baucher. He didn't look like he was enjoying himself. It was not his kind of music. He needed his Too $hort, "So You Want to Be a Gangster."

I saw Mr. Case in the corner, one of the chaperones. It was really late to drive back to Angels Camp.

The next song was a fast song called "Bricklayer." Everyone got into it, even the jocks, and a small mosh pit formed. I got into it too. In the pit, bodies hit each other and there was sweat. It was tight and hot. I was behind Brent but he didn't know. I jumped and our bodies collided. And again, in the hot, sweaty circle.

From the side, Mr. Case watched with his crossed eyes.

Jack-O'

I sit in the driver's seat of my grandfather's old DeVille. It is night out and cool. Me and Joe, we just sit.

We're out in front of the Unified Palo Alto School District office, a dead one-story building where old people work. I think of all the boring English teachers I have ever had, and I think they were all born in this building.

We sit here because it's dark, and there are no lights outside this building. We're stopped for no reason except that the night is still going and we're drunk, and who wants to go home, ever, and this spot is as good as any to just sit in the shadows and let life slow.

My window is cracked, just a bit, and the air plays on my

forehead. I often think about driving off the side of freeway overpasses, just plunging Grandpa's old blue boat through the cement guardrail. The sculpted posts crumbling about me and Grandpa's blue machine: a great moment of metallic explosion and heavy ripping and jerking and then release: a soft, slow dive of arcing color through the windshield, into a hard second of impact, just before the black. What an adventure lies behind one quick turn of the steering wheel. A great screaming, and then, slip away.

Joe and I sit and stare at the wall of the building. The building is beige, but the shadows make it shadow-color. Joe smokes. His window is all the way down, and he breathes his smoke out the black gap.

There is not much to talk about with Joe because he's such a moron. I don't know what he thinks he is, or why he thinks he exists. I guess in some people's lives, no one tells you what to be, and so you be nothing. In the olden days you were born into it, all decisions made, and you farmed until you died, or cleaned the royal toilets.

I guess they didn't have toilets. Just stuck their asses out and shat in the moat. But someone had to wash out the hole.

"If you lived in the olden times, what would you do?" I ask Joe.

Joe has to think about it. He is large, and his weight spreads from his belly across the seat, like it was a plastic sack full of liquid, rolling in layers upon itself.

"Which olden times?" he asks, and it's like a boar's grunt, a deep thing, from the thick part of his throat.

"Like, King Arthur, with knights and horses."

Fat-ass thinks. I can hear it, like rust-flaked gears groaning slowly into motion, even smell it, yellow smoke emanating from his skull.

"I'd be the king," he says.

"You can't be the king," I say. "No one is king. That's like winning the lottery."

"If I went back, I'd be king. And I'd fuck every virgin in the kingdom."   .

"You can't be king, asshole. You can't even be *duke*. The fact that you even said that shows you're not royalty. You're a peasant."

"Whenever people time travel, they go back and they are friends with the king, or they *are* the king."

"Because those are stories. When people tell stories, they're *always* about the king; it's Aristotle crap. But it's not *real*."

"Neither is time travel."

"There are very few kings, and you certainly wouldn't be one of them."

"Fuck you."

"Fuck you, Joe, you're an idiot."

"You're an idiot."

"I know," I say. And I am. I am friends with a slug, and my other friends are pigs and wolves. I never make friends with nice things, just the shit.

"If you were king, I'd kill myself," I say.

Joe sucks off his cigarette. It looks like the point of a golf tee in his fat, clenched paw.

He looks at me and the blue shadow-smoke drifts over the gate of his teeth like fog over a graveyard.

"Then you better die, mo'fucker, cuz I'm the king round these parts."

He smiles with rotten teeth like busted shingles, all climbing over each other, and I think, Why don't you get some braces, motherfucker, and brush those dang things? But I don't really think about that too much because I'm thinking about something else, or at least getting ready to do something else, or already doing . . .

And before I even know it, or can enjoy the new look on Joe's face, like a blubbery peekaboo face, so surprised, I'm driving us right toward the vague beige shadow-filled wall, and I can only see and hear Joe's voice for a second, a high-pitched thing that cracks for just a second, and for that second I'm with his voice on a plateau in the black of space, wherever it is that noise cracks like that, and decibels live, and then it's gone because there's the metal sound so loud and it's how I had always planned it to be, crunching, and a jerk, and the front of my head fills with the cold hollow sinus pain, the surprise punch in the nose that takes you back to childhood, and there's an immediate link to every other time you ever had your nose hit, by a ball, by a head, by your own knee, and after the surprise, it doesn't go away; but I'm still there and the tires behind me are screeching because my foot is still on the gas, and the car has gone a ways into the wall but it ain't going any farther, and I look over at fat shit, and there is blood rolling out of a slice in his forehead, and some blood coming out of his mouth, and I think that it's from the head gash until I see one of those teeth is now a black gap and he looks like a fat something-awful: hockey-player-pumpkin-cartoon-shithead, and he says, "Why the fuck did you do that, Manuel?"

I laugh like crazy, a laughter that explodes like popcorn, because he looks so fucking silly, and because my name isn't even close to Manuel. That's his brother's name.

Joe just looks at me with that stupid look, covered in flowing blood, going onto his shirt like ketchup randomness, so much messier and more random than I could ever plan.

But I did paint those swirls, because I drove Grandpa's car into the wall.

For six months I drove around town with that busted car. The front was smashed. I replaced the lights, but they were crooked and looked in different directions like Peter Falk's glass eye and real eye. I didn't care, and the cops didn't catch me or pull me over. For a while.

I'm at school and when I pass Joe in the breezeway, I say, "Hey, Jack-O', we doing this thing tonight?" because we're friends again.

"Yeah," he says. "Hector has the good shit."

Everyone calls Joe "Jack-O'" now because he didn't get a replacement tooth. He kept the hole because he thinks it makes him unique, and he stopped being mad at me after he figured out he wanted the gap, and then we would laugh about me being so crazy driving into the wall, and I smile when people bring it up, but really it was a failure. If only I had driven right through into some other reality, but the DeVille was sturdy, and yes, it was busted in the front, but not really as much as it could have been, and not so much that my parents got too suspicious when I said that another car backed into me.

Now me and Jack-O' are driving down the dark 280 freeway. Me and fat boy cruising. And I think about that missing tooth, and that gap, and how there was never a gap in that place before, and about three dimensions, and how the gap was on the inside of his mouth unless he opened his mouth, and how things, shapes, folded in on themselves, and four dimensions, and if time is variable, then how do I vary it, and why do I want to? Because everything just focuses in on me and I hate it.

"If you were an Egyptian, what would you do?" I ask Joe.

"Don't start this shit again, Michael."

"Remember when you called me Manuel?"

"I never called you Manuel, idiot. I would be Pharaoh."

"No, you're too fat. Pharaohs are skinny," I say.

"I don't want to be an Egyptian: pyramids and mummies and shit, and sand, and all that, fuck it, it's boring, man. I would be an Aztec, or a Mayan, like my peeps, and I'd cut your fucking heart out, homes."

Joe is Mexican. His skin is an ashy light brown and his lashes are heavier than mine, and he has short, fat eyebrows and shit brown eyes, and thick hair that flops about his fat pumpkin head.

I wish I was Mexican, or Hebrew, I mean Jewish, I mean Israeli, or Mexican Jewish, or Mexican Jewish gay, because it can be so boring being you sometimes, and if you were the most special thing like that, it could be really great, but maybe some people say the same thing about you, and you want to tell those people: "No, you're stupid, it's no fun being me."

"Maybe we should try it," I say.

"Michael, I'm serious, don't do something crazy just because we're talking about your olden-time things again. Just let me the fuck out if that's what you're thinking."

"No, man, I'm just saying that maybe those Mayans were onto something. Maybe if we take someone's heart out and sacrifice it, then something special will happen."

Joe looks at me like he wants to figure me out, and I know that he can't figure me out because he isn't laughing and he isn't arguing, he is just staring.

"Maybe we could take *Hector's* heart," I say.

We are going to see Hector over at Foothill, the junior college. He lives near there and sells us shit, and we're supposed to meet him in the corner of the parking lot. Hector isn't a scary guy, he has a nice-guy face, but he could probably fuck somebody up if he wanted to.

"Hector would fuck you up," says Joe.

"Not if I stabbed him in the stomach," I say, and I'm reaching under my seat with my left hand as I say this, and I pull out a foot-long kitchen knife and then I point it at Joe while I'm still driving.

"Fuck you, Michael. Fuck you, Mike-*al*!" He screams and I laugh because he has funny inflections when he gets excited. "Why do you have to be like this?" he says. "Why do you have to be Jack the Ripper psycho? Why do you have to be so crazy? I just want to buy some weed, I don't want to kill anyone, and I don't want to take their heart!"

"You said you wanted to, *puta,* so I'm just saying, then let's *do* it!" I'm talking with a phony accent.

"Don't call me *puta,* bitch! And put that fucking knife down! And watch the road!"

I poke the knife at him, at his fat stomach, lightly poking at it with the tip of the knife, but he's wearing a puffy North Face jacket, so it doesn't stab him.

"Stop it!" he says.

I love driving down an empty dark freeway, lit up intermittently by the lights at the side of the road, and when I see the lights, I think of all the little worlds out there, all the little animals living in their habitats out there, and how we could pull over and have an adventure at any one of these forgotten pockets of the world, just nothing zones, backwash refuse property in the wake of the great freeways, and I like passing all of them, racing down the freeway, like a tunnel into the night, and racing but still being able to carry on a whole action scene with Joe, and I think it is like life because I am racing, and time is pushing me forward and it's not going to stop and I will have a few passengers in the vehicle with me, and it's either enjoy the scenery together, or listen to some music we both like, or maybe just have a little poking knife game because you want to know if the other person is really there.

We smoke with Hector and get so high. Finally he has sold us some good shit. We smoke out of his mini dragon bong, out in the lightless corner of the Foothill parking lot. It's a pretty great spot—you just walk up the hill a little ways, and it's under some weeping willows, and there is a small stream, and brick buildings, and a faux altar constructed out of stones.

We smoke more and we cough every time. I think about the little dragon that the bong is and I so wish that dragons were real, because it would mean that none of this shit was the end of everything, because this world sucks, and even if you are high it only lets you escape a little bit, it lets you escape enough that you know there could be something better, but it won't let you *into* that place; like standing on the cloudy threshold of heaven and seeing something so bright and tantalizing and warmy-womby feeling but not being able to enter, just feeling the heat a little on your face, and you want to cry and smile, but instead you just stare and you can't do anything.

"Hector," I say. I am lying on the altar thing and staring up through one of the willows, whose drooping, arcing branches are like jagged fissures in the sky. Hector is sitting against the base of the willow's trunk. "Would you rather be the pope or Pablo Escobar?"

Hector doesn't think long.

"Escobar, bitch, he gets to have all the fun."

"Pope gets to live in the Vatican, see Michelangelo all the time," I say.

"Escobar," says Joe. He is superhigh. He hogged more of the weed than Hector and me and he is hunched like a pile of trash against the base of the altar. His head hangs forward like a sleeping mule's.

"Shut up, Joe," I say. "We know what you want. You want the knife."

"What knife?" says Hector.

"This *puta* wanted to cut out your heart with this knife," I say, and hold up the knife for Hector to see. It reflects a little in the dark.

"If you try, I will fucking kill you, homes," Hector says to Joe. It seems like he's angry, but he's too tired and high to get really angry.

"I didn't say I wanted to . . . ," says Joe, but he doesn't finish.

"Fuck you, lard-ass," says Hector, and Hector and I laugh, and Joe shifts a little because he is angry, but he is too lazy to get up, so he just shifts around.

He's still looking at the ground, but he says, "No, Hector, this fucker is always asking me stupid questions and trying to kill me. He wanted to cut out your heart, homes. That's how I lost my tooth."

"No," says Hector. "You lost that because you are Jack-O' the jackoff."

Me and Hector laugh.

Then we all sit for a while not saying anything. I can feel their mind-killing slime thought rubbing on me and corroding me, and killing me.

"Hector," I say.

"Yes," he says without looking up.

"Would you rather be gay or be a girl?"

He chuckles a little. Hector can be cool sometimes. Sometimes he is wise.

"Neither," he says.

"Just saying," I say. "If you had to choose because a genie said so, what would you choose?"

Joe, still looking at the dark dirt, says, "Both of 'em still have to suck dick."

"Exactly," says Hector. And Joe laughs a little. A chuckling pile of trash below me.

"Would that be so bad?" I say. "Don't you ever get jealous of those girls in pornos that get to be on their knees in the middle of all those dicks?"

"Are you fucking serious?" says Hector.

"Don't," says Joe. "This faggot is always asking stupid questions and giving stupid answers; he don't mean it."

"No," says Hector. "This faggot is serious." He's looking at me now, I can tell.

"Yeah," I say. "Don't you like the idea of an around-the-world blowbang?"

"I like to have a girl suck my dick, but I don't want to *do* it," says Hector.

"Me neither," says Joe, but he is mumbling.

"Why not?" I say. "What's the difference?"

"What's the difference?" says Hector. "Because I am going in, and she is being got inside of."

"And why is one better? Why does going inside make you better? Aren't you, like, on her turf inside her, isn't she in control of you? Like a mommy with her little baby making him feel good?"

"Because," says Hector. But he doesn't say anything else.

*　*　*

On the way home Joe and I are driving down the empty free-way. It's like two thirty in the morning and we're still pretty high, and if I look up, directly at the road lights above us, I can see kaleidoscopic rainbows building and turning on top of each other in the core of the bulbs.

And I feel like I'm remembering all this from somewhere, but I'm not sure where, and everything is a little hazy, and I remember that there is an angel named Michael, and he had a flaming sword, and . . .

And I say to Joe, "Let's drive the wrong way down the other side of the freeway."

Joe is almost asleep, but he says, "Wha?" and I can see the black gap just to the left of the center of his mouth.

"I'm going over to that side," I say.

And I think of the olden times, when knights would aim huge lances at each other and you would *feel* that when it hit you, *feel* that force of the momentum of the horses' pumping, channeled into the lance, and for a second you might know that you were really alive. And a little ways down the freeway there is a gap in the center barrier, and I turn the wheel and cross over.

Yosemite

The drive up to Yosemite was long. My father played Bach the whole first half. We drove through Milpitas, Pleasanton, Dublin, Manteca, Escalon, and Oakdale. We had been to Yosemite before with my mom, but that was when it was snowing. There wasn't going to be snow this time and it was just me and my dad and my brother.

At the turnoff for the Old Yosemite Road, the sun turned tangerine and my dad took out the Bach and put in a tape of his meditation lady. My brother and I chanted with her using funny voices, but that lasted only a few minutes, then we were quiet again. My dad drove and hummed quietly to himself. My brother and I would trade the front seat at every rest stop. I was two years older, but I got carsick more easily, so I got the front longer. I had been in the front since East Oakdale. The Old Yosemite Road was crooked and my dad drove slower. Soon the sky was getting gray, but there was purple above the mountains. My brother was asleep in the back. He was slanted over with his face in all the puffy jackets.

"Dad, can I turn the heat up?"

"Yup." I did and cupped my hand over the grate until it was too hot and I pulled it away. I wasn't tired even though it was dark outside and we'd been driving for hours. I leaned forward but my seat belt held me, so I undid it and leaned again and picked up my father's old, thick Bible with pages falling out and a rubber band around it.

"Put your belt back on," he said.

"I know," I said. I clicked it in place. "I was just picking this up."

"My Bible."

"I know," I said. "Why are the lines colored?" There was yellow, and pink, and green highlighter, all faded, all over the pages.

"Those are passages I like."

I asked him why.

"Because they help me." I read a little. *Surely goodness and mercy shall follow me all the days of my life.* It meant nothing. I closed it.

"You go to church?"

"No," he said. The lady and the people on the meditation tape were chanting softly.

"Why do you have the Bible?"

"I just open it when I get in the car. Whatever page it opens to, I read."

"Why?"

"I told you, it helps me."

I put the rubber band back around the leather cover and held the thick thing in my lap. We went through a town with only a few lights and my dad slowed. The headlights bounced off some signs into my eyes. One said Yosemite thirty miles. Then we were on the windy part going up the mountain. The tape came to the end and my dad ejected it and left it sticking out of the player. It was white. The Bible tried to slip down my leg and I held on to it.

"Adam and Eve," I said.

"Yup," my dad said.

"Noah."

"Yup."

"Moses, Abraham. Jesus, David. The flood, killing the ram, the plagues, first there was light, then darkness, then water, then land, then the Garden of Eden."

"Where did you learn all that?"

"At Sunday school, where Mom takes us."

"Unity?"

"Yeah." We got quiet as we wound up the mountain. The car went so close to the sides and there wasn't always a barrier. Last time we did this part of the drive in the dark too and I hated it. I secretly held on to the side of the door with my right hand. There were pennies in the handle and I pushed them back and forth in the holder with my index finger. Dad's AA medallion was in there too.

I hoisted up a little and tried to look over the side of the cliff but there were just trees and black, and there was too much back and forth, so I sat back. I tried to pretend we were going into the Misty Mountains and there were goblins around us, but I felt dizzy and I stopped. We kept going and I couldn't sleep, all I could do was sit there.

"You want to know what my dad did with me when I was little?"

"What?" We were talking quietly because of my brother in the back.

"Nothing." He laughed a little. "My dad was a son of a bitch."

We were quiet for a while.

"Why do we go to Yosemite all the time?"

"We've only been a couple times. You don't like it?"

"No, I do. I like the Ahwahnee. But why do we go?"

"I guess because nature makes me feel good. And I want to spend time with you and Alex."

"Because you love us?"

"Yeah, because I love you, and I've missed you."

At the Ahwahnee there was no one around. We parked and followed the footlights along the stone path. My dad carried Alex in one arm and his suitcase in his other hand. I followed with my heavy backpack. The lady at the desk gave my dad a card key and I followed his footsteps down the red carpet with the boxy Indian designs.

In the room, my dad lay Alex on one of the two beds and told me to get into my pajamas. He got some things from his suitcase and went into the bathroom, then the water started running. I took off my shoes and socks and jeans and put on my gray sweatpants and took my toothbrush into the bathroom. I was barefoot and the floor was cold. My dad was in his T-shirt, sitting on the toilet in the corner.

"You should knock."

"Sorry, I heard water."

"It's okay. Brush your teeth." I did and looked only at myself in the mirror. "There's some toothpaste in my toiletry bag there." The square black bag unzipped around the whole side and opened like a mouth. There were two gray Bic razors, and a black and red can of shaving cream that said Barbasol, and a small white and green tube of toothpaste with a Roman column on it. The toothpaste was grainy on my brush and chalky in my mouth. If I looked at the border of the mirror I could see a slanted version of my dad wiping. He stayed on the seat and put the toilet paper between his legs. I always stood up to do it. He wiped for a long time and I mostly looked in my own eyes. Then he was behind me.

"If you brush like that you're going to ruin your gums."

"No I'm not."

"Do it like this." He took his brush and did strokes in only one direction at a time, starting from the gums he went down on the top teeth and then up on the bottom teeth. My dad's teeth were long and nice, except one was a little yellow. He also had heavy eyelids that made him look a little evil.

We went to bed. I lay in the bed with Alex but he didn't wake up. My eyes got used to the dark and I wandered them down the red band of Indian patterns at the top of the wall.

The design was like one long zigzagging tunnel. The room was dark and quiet and full of bodies and I fell asleep.

In the morning we ate in the great hall. The walls were made of stone and there was a fire in the huge stone fireplace in the center. The pillars around the room were huge, made out of real trees.

"Pancakes are good for hiking," my father said. "Try to eat all of them." I tried. I had pancakes and orange juice and hot chocolate and Alex had French toast and hot chocolate and my father ate scrambled eggs and bacon and black coffee. It was all stuff that we didn't usually eat; we usually had cereal at home. There were also little circular plastic jelly containers with pictures of fruit on them, dewy orange slices, a huge glistening strawberry, two raspberries, side by side, plump and wet. I didn't have any toast because of the pancakes, but I lined the jellies up at the top of my plate. Five colorful circles.

"Alex only ate half of his French toast," I said. Three halves of the French toast were soaked in a swamp of syrup.

"He's smaller."

"Why do I have to eat all my pancakes?"

"You don't. But they're good for energy. That's what hikers do, they eat a bunch of carbohydrates and your body keeps them inside as spare energy when you need it. If we're going to go to Yosemite Falls, then you'll need your energy."

"Can we go down the waterfall?" said Alex.

"No, stupid, you'd die," I said.

"Don't say that. Yes, you would die. The waterfall is very powerful and there are rocks at the bottom. But every once in a while someone gets trapped in the current at the top and they go over by accident."

"And they die?" said Alex.

"Yup."

"I don't want to die," said Alex.

"*Everyone* dies," I said.

"I'm not going to."

"You have to," I said. "You're going to freakin' die."

"Chris, stop." My dad didn't get loud but he took my hand and squeezed. "Alex," he said to my brother. "You might have to die, but it will be okay." Alex shook his head. "Dying isn't bad, it's just another trip. Like our trip here, to Yosemite. It's like going to another Yosemite."

Alex said, "I hate Yosemite and I hate dying." My dad was done with his eggs and had only half a piece of bacon left neatly at the side of his plate. He had put his knife and fork in the center to signal that he was finished. I put my knife and fork the same way on top of the last downy pancake.

My dad sipped his coffee then put the mug down and said, "I know you boys don't like coming to Yosemite. But I think when you're older you'll appreciate it. I never had a place like this when I was young. And if you really don't like it, we never need to come again. Okay?"

"I want to never come again," said Alex.

"I like Yosemite," I said.

"You can go on the waterfall and die," said Alex.

"Shut *up*," I said. I mashed one of his French toasts with my thumb. Alex whined and it looked like he was going to cry.

"Alex, stop. Chris, stop." We both sat still. "Listen. Neither of you is going to die for a very long time. I promise. And when you do, you can go anywhere you want. It doesn't have to be Yosemite. It can be any place."

"Round Table," said Alex. He meant Round Table Pizza.

On the trail we walked in a line. I was last. We had our puffy jackets on but it wasn't too cold. Mine was brown and lighter brown, Alex's was red and blue, and my dad's was all blue, bigger and less puffy. I told myself brown was better than red and blue.

The sun was low and shot shafts of gold at an angle through the trees. From far away I could see insects and atmosphere dancing, but when I walked through the light it was warm and the insects were gone. The ground was dry. No one was around. It was just us walking.

Our first stop was supposed to be a bunch of caves. My dad pointed up off the trail and we walked up an incline. After a bit, as we walked up the hill, I could see some people standing in front of the caves. When we got closer, I saw that they were a man and a woman in their thirties, wearing shorts and hiking boots and backpacks. The man had light curly hair like mine but his was down to his ears, and the woman had long, straight brown hair. Her legs were thin like a horse's, and on her knee there was a purple brown scab.

"How's it going?" my dad said.

"Not bad," the man said. "Some candles here." We walked up closer and saw that there was a large circle of white candles in the dirt. The circle was large enough for a person to lie in the middle. "There's another one in there," the man said and pointed up toward the cave. My father said nothing, but he took Alex's hand.

Not long before, I had gone to see *The Little Mermaid* with my mom and Alex at the Old Mill Theater. Seeing movies was one of our traditions. In the middle of the movie I got up and went to the bathroom. On the way back I looked into another theater and saw a few minutes of a movie called *The First Power*. Lou Diamond Phillips was in it. I loved him as Chavez in *Young Guns* so I watched. I knew that it was about the devil and I wasn't supposed to watch. The killer had tied up a woman and put her in the middle of a circle of candles. She was gagged and scared. The killer told her to relax and said he was going to say his prayers backward.

"Heaven, in art which father our are father which art in Heaven." I left and went back to *The Little Mermaid* but I couldn't forget what I saw.

My father didn't let us look at the candles in the cave, so we kept walking. He held Alex's hand and I walked a little behind them. My father and brother both had straight brown hair. The sun was above us and it was hotter. My dad took off his jacket and I took off mine. Alex took his off and we stopped to wait for him to tie it around his waist, but he couldn't do it so my dad carried it for him.

The next stop was El Capitan. It was a tall, boxy mountain that shot straight up out of the ground. In my mind I always thought of it as yellow-orange because I thought of all the mountains in colors: Half Dome was white and gray; Mount Lyell was green; Mount Dana was pink; Matterhorn Peak was blue; but up close El Capitan wasn't yellow-orange, it was just dirty white and chalky.

"Look at that tree," my dad said. It was a tree with reddish bark. High up, some of the branches had been ripped away and in places the bark was skinned off revealing the pale insides. "That's fresh. It's from rocks falling off the mountain."

There was a little stream going almost next to the base of the mountain. My dad gave us time to explore on our own. I told him I didn't want any rocks to fall on me and he promised that they wouldn't. I had nothing to do so I found a place with some sun and I sat with my back against the mountain. I took my shoes off and let my feet feel the air. The water was very close and it trickled and sparkled. From somewhere close I could hear my brother's voice, high and demanding, and my father's voice, deep and calming.

Sitting in the sun I felt empty. I was a black center in the middle of all the nature. I was nothing but I could do anything. I could fill myself with anything. I said a prayer. I asked God that I would never be like my father. I told God that I didn't want to have sons. I said that if I died I would like to have done something good before that happened. I prayed that my brother would die, and then I took it back.

Later, on a large, flat oval rock we had our lunch. The hotel had packed us sandwiches and Cokes. I had turkey on wheat with sprouts and cranberries. It was the best sandwich I'd ever eaten. The Coke washed it down and the sugar stuck to my teeth.

*   *   *

To get to Yosemite Falls we walked through a very green and wet part of the park. The ground was full of mud and damp needles. All the rocks were wet and had a blue gloss. Soon the noise of the falls started growing, and after a while the sound was all around us. A steady rush of horror saying, "You are small and insignificant," and getting so loud that you just wanted to see to get it over with and get out of there. Some people were walking back from the falls toward us. A couple with dark hair and dark clothes. They said nothing as they passed.

The three of us, we three Petersons, walked in a line toward the noise, my father in the center. We had our puffy jackets back on and there was a mist around us. The mist wet our faces as we continued toward the center of the roar. It felt like something was pushing us back but my father kept pulling us forward. The trees were green and black over us, like the arched ceiling of a church.

Then we came out from under the trees and there was a huge rock face and in the center, a cataract, white and gushing, implacable and steady in its furious rush over the side. It was a violent slice of movement in the stolid graphite-colored rock front, and the scene was all glazed over by the shifting atmosphere of mist. The waterfall was farther than I imagined, but the sound roared in a chorus that echoed and reechoed without end. It felt like there were speakers just below us projecting the rushing noise, so loud and close when the waterfall was so far.

We stood for a minute and then made our way up the damp

path to a wooden bridge that spanned the river. At the base of the bridge, the waterfall sent itself smashing on the rocks. It was even louder here, as if we were in a cave of sound. The waterfall was a mystery. It was water and rock and river and time and noise. Is the water the waterfall? I wondered. Or the rock formation that makes the waterfall in that way? Or the combination? You could take a photo of the waterfall, but the particular water captured in the picture would never flow over again.

An old man walked over the bridge. He had on a translucent blue raincoat with the hood up and pulled tight around his face so that only his eyes and nose were showing through the opening. We asked him to take a picture of us and he did, with our backs to the railing of the bridge and the waterfall behind us. Alex was in my father's arms.

The way back felt too far. I knew my father had kept us out too long. We had to walk back past El Capitan. The sun was going down behind the tall, square mountain and there was an orange glow bending around one edge. My dad had my brother on his shoulders and I was dragging my feet. After a while, we left the footpath and walked along a larger dirt road. My father said we were almost back to the hotel, but he had been saying that for a long time. A little off the road there were the remains of the wall of an old stone house. Next to the wall was the wasted foundation. Behind this was another foundation with brick remains ringing its sides. The sun was almost gone.

We walked more. I didn't want to go any farther. Yosemite

was hell. Then, ahead, we saw some burning. As we got closer we saw that there were large burning piles of leaves just off the road. I walked ahead of my father and brother to look at the piles. They were on a stretch of dirt so that the fire wouldn't spread, but the flames went really high. There were five piles about twenty-five feet wide, all taller than I was and the flames leaped taller than my dad. Many of the leaves and branches and sticks had thorns on them and I thought that they might have been poison ivy or poison oak. When I was across from the second burning pile I saw something large and white through the smoke. I walked to the edge of the road and saw that it was a human rib cage. I didn't see a head, but the ribs were very clear, like a corset. I ran back.

"Dad, there's a skeleton over there." My dad put my brother on the ground and told us to wait. He walked to the piles and stood over where the skeleton was. He stood there for a while and then came back to us and put my brother back on his shoulders. "Let's go. A mountain climber must have fallen off the mountain. The animals got to him. It's okay, come on, let's go." We quickly walked past the piles. "Don't look," my dad said, but I did. The pointed ends of the white ribs in the orange light of the fire.

On the way back my father hummed the meditation songs. My brother cried quietly and my father bounced him gently and said it was okay, it was just a hiker that had an accident. He hummed again, and I walked by his side and held his hand. The fire was far behind us, but it still felt close. My footsteps crunched and I didn't want to be on the ground. It was hard to see and for ten minutes in the dark he hummed to us.

Then we were back at the hotel. We took our jackets off and my dad said, "We're stinky boys. We're all going to take showers. Then we'll order room service, okay? Who's first shower?" Nobody spoke. My brother and I sat on the bed. Alex said, "Can we call Mom?"

"No, it's too late to bother Mom."

I said, "Dad, call the police."

My dad picked up the phone.

"Can I have the ranger service, please? Thanks . . ." He waited a bit and we watched. "Hello, I was out walking with my boys near El Capitan and we came across some burning piles. Next to the piles there was a skeleton, I think it must have been a climber that fell off the mountain. . . . No, the animals got to him. . . . Yeah, they even went through the sheathing on the bones. . . . No, no head. No arms either. But there were feet. . . . Yes, they looked human to me . . . sure . . ." Then he waited with the phone to his ear. I was glad we were together because it felt like the world outside was full of murder. Then he was talking again. "I see. . . . Oh, really. Um, hmmm . . . interesting, okay, thank you very much. Yes, the Ahwahnee, room 213, Peterson. Yes, okay, thank you very much." He hung up the phone. "It sounds like it was a bear."

"I saw, it was human," I said. "It was real, I saw."

"I know, but the rangers said it was a bear. It was getting too friendly with the people because people were feeding it, so they had to shoot it."

"It was a *bear*," Alex said.

"Shut up, you didn't even look," I said.

"Don't worry, Chris, I thought it was a person too."

"But why would they shoot the bear if it was being friendly?"

"Because a bear's idea of friendly is different from ours. Bears just want food, so they'll kill you if you have it."

My brother took the first shower and then my dad. He came out with a towel around his waist. He was pale and thin. Before I went in I told my dad I wanted a cheeseburger for dinner. The water was only warm. I lathered the soap in my hands and rubbed it under my pits and around my neck and then down across my chest and ribs and crotch. Then I did my legs and feet and then my crack. When I was lathering my face the water got cold so I danced in place while I washed off the soap. I didn't wash my hair.

After I dried off I put on my sweatpants and T-shirt in the bathroom and went into the main room. The food was there and we sat on the two beds and ate from the table on wheels. We all had burgers and Cokes. The cheeseburger was thick and the cheese was salty and good. The burger was so thick I could hardly fit the first bites in my mouth, and the tomatoes and onions squeezed out the back. My brother had a regular hamburger. He put tons of ketchup on all his hamburgers; I used mustard only because I was more mature. My dad put mustard on his, but spicy mustard made with white wine. He said all the alcohol was cooked out so it was okay for him to eat it.

After dinner my dad put the table outside the door. While he was out my brother and I started jumping on the beds, then we started jumping over the gap between the beds.

"Hey, guys, settle down, settle down, I want to tell you

something." We stopped jumping and I sat on the edge and Alex lay on his stomach. My dad sat on the edge of his bed where he had sat while he was eating.

"Do you guys know how babies are made?"

"I think so," I said.

"How?"

"The husband and wife get naked in a bath together."

"Sick," said Alex.

"Who told you that?" my dad said to me.

"Beatrice." Beatrice was my best friend, a French girl that lived down the street. We had had chicken pox at the same time, and watched *The Dukes of Hazzard* together and the movie *Time Bandits*. She had itched her chicken pox and got an indent between her eyes, like she'd been hit by a miniature cork.

"Beatrice is wrong," said my dad. "Yes, the man and the woman get naked but they don't have to get into the bath. Usually they do it in a bed."

"Why?"

"Because it's comfortable there."

"Why are they naked?" said my brother.

"Because the man needs to put his penis in the woman's vagina."

"*What?*" I said. My brother was squealing and squirming on the bed beside me.

"When two people are in love, that's what they do. It's not gross if you love each other . . ."

"You and mom?" I said.

"Yes." My brother was really going crazy with the squeals then, rolling onto the floor. My dad and I started laughing.

"You did that for me and Alex?" I said. My dad nodded. "Yes."

"That is gross," I said and my brother repeated me, *"gross!"* Then I asked, "Do you still do it?"

My dad took a long time to answer.

Then we all got ready for bed. I let my dad and my brother brush their teeth first and then I went in there alone. I tried to brush the way my dad had told me to, but it didn't feel right so I just brushed in my old way. The bear had ribs like I had ribs. Underneath had been lungs, and a stomach and a heart and they all got burned away.

Acknowledgments

My favorite people are teachers. I have learned tons about writing from Amy Hempel, Mona Simpson, Gary Shteyngart, Ben Marcus, Michael Cunningham, Catherine Texier, Jenny Offill, Darcey Steinke, Joshua Henkin, Jonathan Baumbach, Stacey D'Erasmo, Tony Hoagland, James Longenbach, Frank Bidart, Alan Williamson, Jonathan Lethem, Victor LaValle, Rick Barot, Ian R. Wilson, A. R. Braunmuller, Mark J. McGurl, Jonathan Post, Lynn Batten, Ellen Tremper, Katherine Hayles, Stephen Dickey, Kenneth Reinhard, and Cal Bedient. They have all been my teachers and friends. Richard Abate for his support. Thank you to Nan Graham and Paul Whitlatch for editing and showing me the way. Dave Eggers and Tyler Cabot too.

PALO ALTO REVISITED: FROM LIFE TO BOOK TO SCREEN

A NEW ESSAY BY JAMES FRANCO

After acting professionally for almost a decade, I wanted something more: a mode of expression that was less dependent on collaboration than film. Literature had always been a passion of mine, but I had dropped out of pursuing an English degree at UCLA years earlier to pursue acting. My girlfriend suggested I try a writing workshop at UCLA Extension. The course, my first actual writing class, was taught by my future friend and publisher, Ian R. Wilson. Ian broke down all the basics of writing: character perspective, structure, dialogue, metaphor, etc. I had been writing for years, but I had never showed my work to anyone; the workshop structure of the class forced me to be responsible about what I wrote because it was *actually going to be read*.

After Ian, I was hooked. I reenrolled at UCLA proper and began studying under great teachers like N. Katherine Hayles, A. R. Braunmuller, Mark McGurl, Cal Bedient, Jonathan Post, Mitchum Huehls, and Mona Simpson. This is when I started writing the stories that would eventually become *Palo Alto*.

I grew up in Palo Alto, California. I went to Paly High School, across the street from Stanford University. When I was in high school I befriended a pale Russian boy named Ivan. He was so pale that except for his eerie light blue eyes he could have been mistaken for an albino. Ivan was crazy wild. When everyone else was experimenting with alcohol and pot, Ivan was going on blackout benders. When I started getting into trouble for similar behavior, I could always look at Ivan and tell myself that I wasn't that bad. During our sophomore year, Ivan got in a fight *every* weekend, and every Monday he would show up to school with black eyes, split lips, and purple welts on his arms. This pattern culminated during a post-prom party (his albino sheen prevented him from ever attending the actual prom) when Ivan, lying on the pavement of a driveway, had his face kicked multiple times as if it were a soccer ball. When I visited him at Stanford Hospital, in addition to his face, he was also being treated for alcohol poisoning. The doctors thought he had been assaulted by a baseball bat. His face was sutured like Frankenstein's monster, and they said if he had been kicked one more time his nose bone would have gone up into his brain and killed him.

After high school Ivan and I lost touch. He had begun losing his mind. He was schizophrenic, and the alcohol had been a way to stave off the rising demons. Around the time I went back to school, I heard that Ivan had jumped off a building in San Francisco and killed himself. It had happened a few years before, but no one had told me about it. There had been only a handful of us who really knew Ivan, and I knew from the way my own memories were slipping away that he would fade for the others as well. I started writing about him. He was going to be the main character in my book. The book was going to be a way to memorialize him, to preserve my memories of him. Eventually other memories took over and the Ivan stories were pushed to the side; like Ivan, his stories didn't work well with others, so the other voices from my youth became the nexus of *Palo Alto*. But the impetus to *remember* was still there.

Eventually the desire to embalm and memorialize my youth turned into something else, and the barometer dial moved to the side of fiction. My hope is that experiences—my own and others'—were transformed and recontextualized so that they became something more than memoir; they became containers for universal experience.

I worked on *Palo Alto* for about four years while I attended classes at UCLA, Columbia University, and Brooklyn College. I wanted the book to be both specific to a time and place but also be universal in the way it spoke about youth and about being human. Teenagers experience so many changes: it is a time full of new physical and emotional sensations. In those years we start to learn who we are, who we want to be, who our friends are. High school is a place where you are forcibly bunched together with different kinds of people, which can be seen as a microcosm of the greater world. Except in high school it seems like there is no escape. When we are older, we usually have some agency to decide whom we want to spend our time with, but high school is the compactor that brings everyone together. In teenagers, emotions are less contained; when we grow older we learn to suppress our feelings. For these reasons, younger characters are great for writers and directors. To teenage characters small events can seem momentous. Great drama can be squeezed out of humdrum situations. And in the end, what teenagers worry about— love, identity, the future—are still the things that adults worry about, so in that sense teenagers can be used as synecdoches for the human condition. It's just that teenagers are a more raw incarnation.

Some of the *Palo Alto* stories are based on experiences I had. Some are based on the experiences of other people, and others I made up. The important thing for me was the way that everything was framed and organized. Even the material based on real experiences was changed because of the way it was inflected and contextualized in the stories. The book is pointedly fiction, and the narrative perspective is that of a young person. It is not supposed to be my unfiltered reflections on youth a decade after the fact. As art, it uses the material of life but transforms it for its own purposes.

When the book was published I naturally thought about a film adaptation—I come from the world of film, after all— but I knew I didn't want to do it myself. There were several reasons for this: I had been collaborating on a bunch of different kinds of projects and appreciated the way that different creative forces working on one project could pull it into unexpected directions; I had been adapting and directing the work of William Faulkner and Cormac McCarthy, and I liked the idea of someone else doing the same to my work. I also knew that if I adapted *Palo Alto* myself it would be bound to my vision, that the work wouldn't grow as much as it could during the transition from page to screen because the sensibility that was already in the book would shape the movie. I knew I wanted someone who shared my sensibility but could also take the material to new places.

I didn't know Gia Coppola very well when I approached her. We had mutual friends and I knew her mother a little. One day I was in Joan's on Third in Los Angeles, reading to my girlfriend and having lunch, and I noticed a young woman come in with her friends. I didn't know it was Gia, but the group caught my eye—they were young, hip, artsy— looking in the deli display and joking around. There was a specific, cool sensibility they had that stuck with me. That night I went to the annual MoCA Gala and there was an after party at this strange venue on Sunset Boulevard, near the old Tower Records, and by coincidence Gia was there with her mother, Jacqui, who introduced us. She embarrassed Gia by saying that she was a huge fan of *Freaks and Geeks,* and then I told Gia I had seen her earlier that day. Gia said she had just graduated from Bard, where she had studied photography. I told her to send me some of her stuff, and that started an email friendship.

Soon after she invited me to a small show of her photographs. The photos had a sensibility that echoed what I was trying to do with my book. The perspective was a way of looking at teenagers through a prism of the fantastic: the cool but vibrant lens that Gia shares with her aunt Sophia, a way of looking at the mundane world of youth, but giving that pedestrian existence the sparkle of dreams. It was looking at that world through the eyes of the teenagers—the way they find their lives at different times extremely boring and extremely exciting. That is what I tried to capture in the book and that is what I saw in Gia's photos.

I have good instincts about people's abilities, and so I called Gia and asked if she wanted to adapt my book. Of course, if anyone had filmmaking in her blood it was Gia Coppola, a child raised on her grandfather's movie sets. She read *Palo Alto* quickly and immediately said she would do it, and that launched the two-year journey transforming the book for the screen.

Gia has a great sense of character, composition, and pace. She knows how to make material seem subtle on the surface but full of emotion underneath. She is a master of creating layers of meaning and feeling, ambiguous energy that elevates the subject from teenage drama into art. She also did a great job of combining and interweaving the stories. The book is a collection of loosely connected stories, but Gia stitched them together in such a way that there is more of an overarching design that is less episodic than the book. If I had directed the film I'm sure I would have gone for the episodic structure, but now I can see that Gia's approach was better for the film. It created an emotional arc with great tension. In fact, I originally planned the book to have more of a connective spine that would link the different voices, à la Faulkner's *As I Lay Dying*; in that book different characters tell their experiences using the first person, but they are also telling the same story. Eventually I dropped my own linking device (the death of a student) because I didn't need it. High school *does* feel like a collection of episodes, so it worked for the book. But movies work differently, and Gia smartly swaddled the material in a tight, unified structure, refashioning it back to a unified design like I had originally conceived.

It is strange to have your work (especially work inspired by your life and people you knew) turned into a film. Performers embody characters who recall aspects of real-life figures. I had no intention of casting people who evoked for me these real-life individuals, but in truth it was eerie how close the actors and their performances came to the ghosts of the originals. It was as if Gia and her team had conjured up the bones of my youth and given them skin and the spark of life.

Gia asked me to play the teacher, Mr. B, who has a relationship with his student. Frankly, I felt uncomfortable embodying this evil character, especially when my allegiances were with the teenagers, but I also wanted to do everything I could to support the movie. I played the guy as well as I could. My insides were saying they wanted me to be with the team of the young people while my outsides took the shape of this compromised adult. Ultimately the book and the movie do just that: they allow me and the audience to inhabit youth, to live out the trials of youth, but through the prism of art. In so doing, the troubled lives of the teenagers I created in these works, dramatic and painful when experienced in real life, but fascinating when refracted in art, take on meaning. They are elucidating, and as the great Werner Herzog says of his own cinema, these experiences, refashioned and played back, are tools for illumination.

PHOTOS FROM THE SET OF GIA COPPOLA'S *PALO ALTO*

CAPTIONS BY JAMES FRANCO

Teddy and Fred. I broke myself in two to create these characters.
The Light and the Dark, one side speaking to the other. And there is
lightness in the Dark and darkness in the Light.

Jack and Gia, children of Hollywood, on their first movie together.
Partners in crime.

One of the things I love about youth—that Gus Van Sant seems to love, Larry Clark seems to love, Humbert Humbert seems to love—is that there is a moment where an innocent beauty can allow a person to do anything and be invincible. Just for a second. And in that second is a glorious, dangerous viciousness.

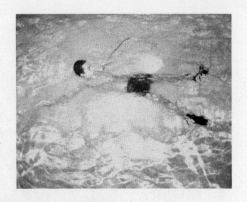

The actors became like River and Keanu in *My Own Private Idaho*, and like the De Niro/Keitel duo in *Mean Streets*. Skateboarding in California is the best

Mike Kelley looked back at high school in his *Day Is Done* show. That's how I like to use high school, as a formal container for the most intense subject matter.

The girls in high school killed me.

Gia Coppola was born to direct. She never knew her father, but as a baby her grandfather would bring her in a basket to his sets and she would sit by the monitor, nursed on the fumes of moviemaking.

Yeah, I got arrested. A lot. At the time I thought I was the unluckiest kid in the world, but now I see that all the trouble led me into the arms of art; in hindsight I'm grateful that I got everything out of my system so that I could stop running and focus on what I loved.

In high school the car becomes a door to the bigger world. It is a home, a haven, a tool, and a weapon. The school is a beehive and the cars are the drones, taking the sweet honey of youth all around.

When you're in high school everything can seem painful: either painfully boring or painfully disappointing. But after high school you can look back on it and see that it was all experience, all vital life, and it can be used to make art.